GHOSTS
OF TIMBER
WOLF

Other books by V. S. Meszaros:

Dead Man's Money
Lone Survivor

GHOSTS
OF TIMBER
WOLF

•

V. S. Meszaros

AVALON BOOKS
NEW YORK

Published by Thomas Bouregy & Co., Inc.
160 Madison Avenue, New York, NY 10016

Library of Congress Cataloging-in-Publication Data

Meszaros, V. S.
  Ghosts of Timber Wolf / V. S. Maszaros.
       p. cm.
  ISBN 978-0-8034-7760-5 (hardcover : acid-free paper)
I. Title.
  PS3613.E878G48 2010
  813'.6—dc22

                                        2009046901

PRINTED IN THE UNITED STATES OF AMERICA
ON ACID-FREE PAPER
BY HADDON CRAFTSMEN, BLOOMSBURG, PENNSYLVANIA

GHOSTS
OF TIMBER
WOLF

Author's Note

Daniel Boone's wife claims, as do historians in general, that Daniel Boone's disappearance into the Kentucky wilderness for two long years was a direct result of this meeting with Dave Merrill at Ford's Trading Post. The present writer is inclined to agree.

Prologue

Before the first rays of morning even began to lighten the autumn sky, the warriors crawled out of their blankets, exhorted by the command of their elders. The cold smoke of a hundred fires still rose from the gray embers that the sages had read the night before. The message had been clear: *Kill the white man. Kill the white man. Kill him! Kill him! Kill him!* It had been repeated on everyone's lips over and over until the Indians had been worked up into a frenzy of hate and jubilation.

The men would split up into two groups. One, on foot, would go to Fort Pitt. The other, on horseback, would go farther afield to Fort Hardin. They would destroy the settlers and anyone else they were lucky enough to meet.

The Indians went gladly about their business, supremely confident of their success. Did not the august ghosts on Timber Wolf Pass exhort them to action? Were the spirits not behind them with every particle of power they possessed?

One tall warrior with long black hair flying about his head and a triple strand of bear claws decorating his thick neck tested his 'hawk. He liked to hear the sound of it cutting the air. The axe would do its work well.

Another buck, handsome and proud, took up his war club. With it he had bashed dozens of heads—Indian and white—for he seemed to agree with no one. He preferred it to the tomahawk.

Both were celebrated and distinguished in their tribes for their fighting abilities. Both looked forward to the coming raids across the river. They were eager to meet the adversary who had enough artistry and cunning to make it a pleasure and honor to kill him in a glorious fight.

Killing men in quantities was enjoyable but would not earn them the accolades they so richly deserved. To kill a great warrior in a great way would earn them smiles of gratitude from the people and rewards from the ancestors who watched over them from Timber Wolf Pass.

It would not be a quick death, however. No. They must find the man who would not flinch when they drove a red-hot knife blade into his flesh. The man who would scoff at death and embrace with a grin the excruciating torture that would drive most men mad. A delicacy for the ancestors to tuck into.

One man. Just one man . . .

Chapter One

Dave Merrill leaned back against the counter on his elbows, chest puffed up importantly, and proceeded to tell everyone listening how he had managed to get back to Fort Pitt alive.

"Musta been about fifty of them red devils on my tail, but all they got was my hat!" He took off the unfortunate item and showed them the two arrow holes. "An inch either way and I'd a been lookin' at my brains," he confessed solemnly.

"If'n ya had any!" one of his friends snickered.

Dave gave this comment the look of attention it deserved. And rightly so. He was one of Maxcy's best rangers, in his opinion. Young and tough and primed for action, he was picturesque standing there in his buckskins. He was a magnificent specimen with his rugged good looks and deep blue eyes snapping with the reckless excitement of the hunt. He was a gosh-darned spellbinder, and didn't he know it! His rakish face brimmed with humor. He was raring to tell them all of his exploits.

He went on to say how one foolish buck who obviously didn't realize with whom he was dealing had jumped into his canoe, tomahawk swinging. "He sure didn't expect me to drive my foot into his brisket, slug him one in the jaw, then throw him out t'other side of the boat, that's for certain sure." He chuckled heartily at his own ingenuity. "Then I kicked another with such brutal force—I got real powerful legs, ya know— why, he landed on his unmentionables. Yessiree, them Injuns fell on me like I was supper. But I tell you now that the day they met up with Dave Merrill, the only thing they et was the bread of sorrow."

He took a stiff drink of cider and grimaced at its tartness. He swallowed it hard, as if it was Satan's own brew, then swiped his sleeve across his mouth with great effect.

"Wow! Fifty Injuns, huh?" one of his friends exclaimed with admiration. The ring of men at Ford's Trading Post listened with varying degrees of belief.

"Heck, that ain't nothin' to what I could tell ya," Dave said modestly, too ready to add, "last month it was more like sixty, but I reckon I can handle any number they throw at me." He sighed heartily. "Yes, sir, there ain't much on this here amazin' earth that can put a scare into Dave Merrill, Injun-whupper!" He finished his story with a flourish. Resting his hand on his long rifle, he struck a pose, well satisfied with the audience's admiration.

Suddenly the door opened, and Jace Cutter came in. "Hey Dave, the widow's looking for you!"

"The widda!" The brave man blanched. He dropped his cup onto the counter, splashing cider on his sleeve. Fear flickered across his handsome face, while his keen hunter's eyes shifted around the place, seeking a fast escape. His knees were flexed for action, ready to run out of there as if he was running on hot coals—the same way he ran from the Indians, as he would often brag.

"You'd better watch it, Dave. You might get away from a passel of redskins but not from a woman!" someone called out.

Another laughed and added, "She's even more dangerous, 'cause she's after more than your scalp. Better use them powerful legs of yourn and skedaddle!"

Dave didn't appreciate this wit at his expense. "I'm gettin' outta here."

"Aw, don't worry," Jace said, pressing a hand onto Dave's shoulder to hold him in place. Grinning, he ordered a drink. "She wouldn't dare come in here." The taproom of Ford's Trading Post, affectionately called The Watering Hole, was a place where the men of Fort

Pitt came to hide from their womenfolk. Females weren't allowed in this inner sanctum by popular vote— the men's. Dave's hide was safe here among his cronies.

"That's right." Dave seemed heartened. He let himself relax, and all his bravado came rushing back. "Why, she wouldn't dare come in here." He settled back more easily against the counter and continued. "Where was I? Oh, yeah. Now, I'm not just lyin' to you about them Injuns. That was a real-live occurrence, that was. You, Henry, why don't ya move a little closer so's you can hear me better? No use you strainin' somethin' to listen." He pointed to a man sitting on the fringe of the crowd. "And I got me plenty more to say." He opened his mouth to proceed.

Just then the door swung wide, and a young woman stood uncertainly on its threshold. Pretty she was, with brown hair and soft brown eyes. She was neatly dressed in calico, and she held her skirts daintily as she finally decided to walk into the room. The men stared in horror, but she didn't seem to care. Instead, her eyes surveyed the crowd till they came to rest on the object of her search.

Dave was flabbergasted. He looked frantically for an escape, but there was none.

"Dave Merrill, I want to speak to you," she said coolly.

The men stifled their laughter and waited around eagerly to watch the fun. Some moved closer to make sure they heard it all.

"Mrs. Wr-Wright!" Dave protested, stammering. "Ya shouldn't come in here. This ain't no place for a lady."

"I don't care. I've been meaning to talk to you for a long time, but you've been avoiding me," she stated flatly.

"No such thing!" he denied strongly.

"Yes, you have, but I'm going to have my say, so you can just stop slinking around and listen."

Dave was forced to. There was no place to run. He began to sweat.

"Ma'am, you got him cornered. You may as well say your piece," someone encouraged her.

She did. "Dave Merrill, you're a pathetic man."

"I am?" He was shocked.

"Yes! Look at you. Thirty years old and you haven't done anything useful with your life."

"I—"

"Be quiet," she commanded. "You go running errands for the colonel and call it work. Any little money you do make from that, you fritter away. You have no proper home, no money saved, and no family. In a few months it will be winter. Oh, I know, the sun is shining now, and you don't want to think ahead. But what will you do then? Every year the winters will be getting colder and colder, and you still won't have a place of your own. If you marry me"—she stumbled self-consciously over those words—"you would at least have a nice cabin, land to give you an income, and someone to share it with." She stopped, waiting for him to say something, but he was speechless.

"Think about it." She put her pretty chin up in the air. "This offer will not be open forever. I thought you were a good, honest man, and I still do. And I think I would make you a darned good wife." She stopped, well aware of the many delighted eyes upon her. "Just think about that." She whirled around and left.

Several moments of silence ticked by. Everyone was awestruck. Then their tongues loosened.

"Woo-ey, Dave, better run for the hills! That's one determined female!"

"Why don't you marry her?" Jace suggested. "She's a good-looking woman. They don't come any better than her. And her farm is real nice."

Everyone had an opinion about it, and all of them gave it loudly and freely in this public forum. Some men urged him to pull up stakes and leave. Others, more daring, urged him to take the plunge.

"I won't!" Dave said, stung. "I'll be damned if I'll be hog-tied and drug to the altar like some poor, dumb animal. I'm a man, and I won't be chased by no woman. I'll do the chasin' if there's any to be done," he announced proudly. "I'm like a young bull buffalo who don't want to be cut down in his prime and made into a dirty old rug for some bossy woman to walk all over. No female is gonna carry me home on her shield."

"Why, she's sweet as can be!" one man protested

hotly. "Last winter my dog got sick, and she took care of it real good. She has fine, gentle hands."

Dave looked at him contemptuously. "I'm not a dog—I'm a man. And men don't go gettin' rushed into anything. When I marry—*if* I marry—I'm goin' to take a good look around first. Then I'll do the choosin' myself. I ain't bein' hurried into nothin' just because the snow starts a-flyin'." He was full of self-importance as he declared this; then he stomped off, slamming the tavern door after him. He had had enough of his comrades for one day.

Monty, one of Dave's friends, came up to Jace as he continued to sip his drink. "How do ya figger, Jace, that the winters are gettin' colder?"

"What?" Jace responded absentmindedly.

"Ya heard the widda. She said the winters are gettin' colder each year. How do ya reckon she knows that? Does she do a bit of trappin'?"

"She's speaking figuratively," Jace said carefully.

"Oh, is that it, then?" Monty said, not understanding. "Figgatively, is it? Well, that explains it, then." There was a long pause. "Thinkin' makes me awful dry. Could ya buy me a drink?"

"No." As Jace Cutter finished his ale in peace, he thought about Angela Wright. He felt sorry for her. A nice-looking woman like her could have her pick, but she had her mind set on Dave Merrill. He shook his head. Frankly, he thought she was too good for Dave.

Making her come in here and practically beg him to marry her—what a cad Dave was.

By the time Jace finished his drink and strolled outside, both the widow and Dave had disappeared. Jace made his way back to his silversmithy and sat at his worktable. But he didn't work. He was still mulling over what had just happened.

On the table lay the pair of scissors he had finished sharpening for Angela Wright. She had been in too much of a hurry today to come pick them up. Jace made an exasperated sound. He winced when he remembered Mrs. Wright's desperate but futile attempt to wrest a proposal of marriage from Dave Merrill—in public yet. Dave had squawked like a turkey with its tail feathers pulled.

Jace figured everyone at the fort would now be talking about Mrs. Wright. It was, after all, an enjoyable bit of gossip. There would be sympathy for her, but there would be talking just the same. If Jace knew Dave, he would check to make sure his tail feathers were still intact, then grab at any excuse to get away from the fort until the storm clouds blew away. Dave couldn't fathom women, and that which man doesn't understand, he fears. Probably by morning Dave would have decamped.

Jace was therefore surprised to see him strolling around the grounds the next morning. He didn't seem to be in any hurry to leave either. On the contrary, he seemed to have recovered his cheerful spirits. Instead of being frightened, Dave was, obnoxiously, rather proud of being pursued.

"Bet I'm the only man hereabouts who had a woman propose to him," he said with a smirk as he came up to Jace. His handsome countenance glowed with self-appreciation.

"She didn't exactly propose to you," Jace pointed out patiently.

"Sure, she did! You was there. Practically got down on her knees," he bragged. "Can't blame her for settin' her sights so high." He flexed his muscles. "Ya know, Jace," he confessed, "I didn't know I was drivin' the poor widda crazy with my own good looks. I plumb didn't realize how much the sight of my manly magnificence put her in such a flutter. Reckon there's plenty more women been eyein' me up with admiration." He cast a look around, as if trying to detect some female in the act of appreciating him. Several women went past and nodded. Dave smiled back warmly, convinced they were hiding a deep and abiding love for him. He turned back to Jace with a wink, as if having proved a point.

"Ya see? Lots of women are hoardin' idolizing thoughts of me. And it's not just my looks or my reputation as a first-class fightin' man," Dave pointed out. "Reckon the widda must be plumb bedazzled by my stories too. Notice how people are always yearnin' to hear more of 'em? Them stories have been spread far and wide, I hear tell."

"Yeah, by you," Jace said, perturbed. Dave laughed heartily while Jace fought to hold on to his temper. "She's got a really comfortable house and good farmland. Be an advantage to any man to own it."

"Nice to own it, but who'd want to work it? All day long in the hot sun. Tied up so's ya don't go nowheres. Plus a bossy woman to keep me at it. Nope, a man's got to have his dignity. Can't let a woman lay down the law. It goes against nature. Why, I recall the time—"

"Mrs. Wright is not bossy. She's very kind." Jace's tone was stiff as he interrupted Dave's ramblings.

Dave peered at him. "You ain't sweet on her yourself, are ya?" he asked, astounded.

"Why are you so surprised? Maybe I am. After all, others might appreciate her even if you don't."

Dave watched him closely. "Oh, I get it. You don't want a noose around your own neck, but you're willin' to twist one around mine."

"Dave!" he ground out between clenched teeth.

"What?" Dave asked smoothly.

"You don't deserve a good woman!"

"I agree. I don't deserve her."

His smugness infuriated Jace. And Jace blew up. "If I were you, I'd marry her before she gets to thinking."

"Thinkin' about what?" Dave asked, falling into the trap.

"Thinking about how little she's getting in return. What have you got to offer any decent woman? No money, no home, not even steady work. Buttons missing on your clothes. You probably have holes in your socks."

Dave curled up his toes automatically, wondering how Jace knew.

"And you need a haircut—and manners!" Jace added. "Why, there are a hundred men who would make a better husband. In fact," he added as inspiration struck him, "if they send those soldiers over from Fort Hardin this winter, the widow won't even bother to look your way. I'll bet she'll be married before a month is up, and she'll have plenty to choose from too. Maybe," he added for good measure, "I'll look her up myself."

He surprised a look of shock, then disbelief, and finally slow anger on Dave's face. With that, Jace grinned back insolently. He strode off, leaving a speechless Dave in his wake. He hoped he'd given Dave something to think about—and worry about.

Jace headed to the tavern, the scene of yesterday's crime.

"G'day, Jace," Ford greeted him, then lowered his voice. "What's Dave gonna do? Attractive woman like Mrs. Wright doesn't have to beg for a husband."

"Apparently she does, if it's Dave Merrill," Jace responded with rancor.

"Can't deny that Dave is young and strong and devilish handsome. Her first husband was an older man, quiet and serious. Can't blame her for wantin' a change."

"I don't blame her. It's Dave's complacent cackling

I can't abide. He was self-satisfied before; now he's even worse. She has him thinking he has depths that haven't been plumbed before. He thinks there's more to him than even he thought there was—and that's plenty! By golly, I've half a mind to go pay my respects to Mrs. Wright myself. Just to see what that cross-eyed buffalo will do!"

"He'd be tickered!" Ford confided.

"Think so?" Jace brightened up.

"Bound to. Isn't there somethin' you're always quoting about vanity and blockheads?"

"Vanity, blockheads, and Dave? That sounds about right," Jace agreed. He was silent for a moment, then banged his fist on the counter. "I'll do it! She gave me some scissors to sharpen. I'll go take them to her tomorrow. She left too quickly yesterday to even inquire."

"And do it up in a parcel," Ford suggested wickedly. "Make Dave think it's a present."

Jace became enthusiastic. "And Penny Holt was talking about sending her some honey. I can take that with me."

Ford nodded.

"Flowers," came a voice next to Jace. Jace turned to look at Captain Tom Maxcy, head of the rangers. He was sweet on Penelope Holt. "Women like flowers," he commented to no one in particular.

Jace smiled. "Good idea. I can pick some on the way."

Ford leaned forward and whispered, "No need. The colonel's wife has a nice garden growing. Maybe she'll let ya have a few roses. They'd make up a fine bouquet."

"She won't," Maxcy said definitely.

"Then take 'em!" Ford urged outrageously. "You can snitch 'em at night. She won't notice," he said—as all men do, misjudging women.

"Good idea." Maxcy nodded. "But be sure to take the red ones, not the yellow," he advised. "She's always going on about those yellow ones coming from her home in Ireland, or wherever she hails from."

Jace straightened up. "I'll pick them before I leave. Dave should be up by that time. I'd like him to see me carrying a bouquet." They all grinned. They liked Dave immensely but enjoyed contemplating his comeuppance with equal pleasure.

"And remember—take the red ones, not the yellow," Maxcy called after Jace as he strode away. Jace waved, and Maxcy turned back to Ford. He frowned. "Or was it the other way around?"

"Don't worry," Ford said, seeing the frown. "Jace'll be miles away afore she finds them roses missin'. If she does."

"She will," Maxcy predicted. "Anyway, I need something to drown my troubles in."

"How about some cider?" Ford knew Maxcy didn't drink much. "It won't drown your sorrows, but it'll sure perk 'em up some." He poured Maxcy a glass. "Any particular trouble worryin' ya now? It couldn't be

Penny Holt, could it? I seen ya flirtin' with her this mornin', and mighty agreeable to it, she looked."

Tom blushed. "No. No troubles there—at least not that I know of. Talk is going around that the Shawnee are gettin' restless. The settlers along the river are mighty nervous."

"There's always talk," Ford pointed out.

"Maybe. We'll have to see." He took another drink. "Then there's Big Bull Tuttle."

"Ah, that one. Used to come in here with his brothers. Clip isn't too bad—not too smart but predictable. But that little one, Vole—he's growin' meaner every time I see him."

"Maybe he is, but it's Bull who's takin' people's land. Got a complaint I have to follow up. Hadley's gone, and Tuttle is claiming his land."

"Bull kill him?"

"Can't prove it. Family back east says he just disappeared." He looked at Ford.

"Yep, people do that around here. Some by choice, some not. Hadley, now, he had himself a good piece of property. Just got done building his cabin this spring and put in crops."

"Yes, real nice of Bull to let him finish." Tom put down his glass. "We'll try to hunt him down. Wherever he's hiding himself now."

"Mind Vole," Ford warned. "He's the kind to sneak up behind ya afore ya know it."

"I hear he's partial to knives," Tom added. "But it's

the Shawnee that really bother me. Never know when they'll get it into their heads to start raiding. Maybe I should have warned Jace about them," he considered, rubbing his chin.

"He'll be fine," Ford said heartily. "Ain't likely he'll run into them tomorrow, is it? Not when he's goin' courtin'." They both laughed.

When he left, Tom stood a moment outside Ford's in indecision. He watched Jace's retreating back as he disappeared into his shop. Taking a step toward it, he was stopped in his tracks by soldiers.

"Colonel Brent wants to see you, sir."

Tom threw another look toward Jace, then turned around. Ford was probably right. Jace would be fine tomorrow. Maybe Tom would have a chance to warn him later.

But Tom was kept busy all day. As he lay down in bed, he remembered he hadn't warned Jace. He frowned and almost got up from his bed. Instead, he lay back. But his dreams were troubled when he finally slipped into sleep.

Chapter Two

Dave Merrill was up early, stoking the fire. When the coffee was done, he wandered to the door and looked out. The fort was abustle even though it was early morning. He raked his fingers through his sun-streaked hair as he tasted the scalding liquid.

Jace Cutter was coming out of his shop, looking clean and shaved and wearing a dark blue coat. A new one—another new one! Dave glanced down at his own worn buckskin jacket and shrugged unconcernedly. He was a fighting man, not a pretty boy. Then his blue gaze sharpened, and he felt a glimmer of disquiet. It was not worry, exactly, and not anxiety, precisely—just a certain conviction that all was not well in his little universe. It soon became apparent why. Jace was carrying flowers.

Dave's mouth hardened. He wondered what that two-headed snake was up to now. He saw Jace stow away two packages in his saddlebag and give them a reverent pat. Jace looked around quickly, almost furtively. When he saw Dave watching him, he waved cheerfully, as if he weren't doing anything wrong at all. Only, Dave knew that he was.

Slamming down his half-drunk cup of coffee, he strode out to see Jace. A few other men had approached and asked Jace where he was bound.

"Hunting," he told them in a voice that was loud and carrying. "Just hunting."

Dave knew it for a lie when he saw the big bouquet of posies Jace was waving about. Did he think Dave was stupid? Dave crossed his arms over his chest and gave Jace a dark look.

"Need any help?" he asked coldly.

Jace grinned. "I don't think so. None that you could offer."

Dave was immediately riled, but he didn't let on. "I'm good at huntin'. Maybe I could give ya a few pointers." His voice was heavy with meaning, which Jace chose to ignore.

"I don't think you could give me any pointers." For a split second Jace's gaze slid over Dave's manly but rather shabby figure. "But I appreciate the offer."

Angry color came into Dave's face. *Widda-stealer!* He didn't know how he contrived to keep from uttering it out loud. Jace was lying! He wasn't going to present them flowers to no bear. Anyways, none that he knew of. He was going to see Angie!

"Which way ya headed?" His voice was clipped. He could be just as cagey.

Jace pretended to consider the question. "North, I think. Yes, north. Here, could you hold this while I mount up?" He thrust the bouquet into Dave's hands and gracefully got onto his horse. Removing the flowers from Dave's hands, he looked at them with longing. "Sweet as the rose," he murmured loud enough for Dave to hear.

"What was that?" Dave took exception to the comment. It sounded presumptuous, particularly since Jace was admiring a large red, velvety rose when he said it. It sounded as if he was already talking to the widda!

"Nothing. Just my romantic spirit bustin' loose." Jace gave Dave a foolish smile. "Wish me luck!"

"I'll do no such a thing." Dave's chest heaved. Jace didn't seem to care.

"Then get out of my way, please. As it happens, I don't need luck." He winked audaciously at his friend's drop-jawed stare. "I'll see you later—much later."

Dave stepped back quickly to avoid the eager horse. The others drifted off, but he stood stock-still in angry silence.

At the fort's gates Jace turned east, not north. Angie lived east of there. That did it. Dave's long stride carried him to his horse, where he quickly saddled up and flew out of there. He was going to see just what Jace was up to. Not that he was thinking of getting mana-cled himself—not a bit. But he still thought it kind of sneaky and low-down dirty for Jace to put himself where he wasn't wanted. Dave figured he had the right of first refusal—sort of—where the widda was concerned.

Disconsolately he rode along, keeping a good distance behind Jace. He hadn't even had a chance to finish his coffee, his stomach was growling with hunger, and he hadn't shaved or washed yet. It was plain discouraging to see Jace looking so fresh and frolicsome. Still, the widda wanted *him,* not Jace. He felt a little better at that thought, but not much.

Cutter was a silversmith and made quite a nice living at his trade. Dave had been working since he was able to walk, but he had no trade of which to speak. He considered Jace's wavy brown hair, clear hazel eyes, and good-looking face. There were some women, he admitted, who might even think him fine to look upon. But then, so was Dave. Didn't he have a piece of looking glass back at the cabin that said so? Anyway, Angie—Mrs. Wright—seemed to think he was handsome. And as for working hard—why, he did. Maybe he didn't have a lot of money to show for it, but he was not lazy, he smoldered. Why, he bet he could work a farm easy—easier than fighting Injuns! Fifty of them! With his bare hands! What more could a woman want?

While Dave's mind was being tormented, Jace, on the other hand, was actually enjoying himself immensely.

Pretending not to see his friend skulking behind him, Jace smothered a grin. He had seen how Dave's beady eyes flickered when he took in the flowers, how the red choler burned in his cheeks at his lame excuse of going hunting. No doubt about it: Dave's dander was up.

Jace enjoyably moseyed along the woodsy trail, holding the bouquet up in front of him like a torch just in case Dave had a hard time seeing. Once he deliberately stopped to refresh the nosegay with some right pretty daisies growing wild in a clearing. From the corner of his eye he could see the fringes on the buckskin jacket twitch with annoyance as Dave ducked behind a tree. He fluffed the flowers a bit and looked at them with admiration.

Just short of the farm where the widow lived, Jace stopped to slick down his hair and brush some imaginary specks of dust from his coat. That would rile Dave, Jace was sure. Dave had little tolerance for those who got themselves "fancied up." Leaving his horse at the hitching post, he went up the wooden steps. In his arms were the two "gifts." Jace knocked loudly at the door.

Dave had sharply watched Jace and his insipid bouquet. He also remembered the mysterious brown parcel Jace had placed into his saddlebag back at the fort. He burned to know what it could be. Now he concluded it was a present of some sort. His mood soured. He couldn't even begin to imagine what Jace had to give Angie Wright, because he didn't know enough about women to know what they'd like. Of course, Jace could afford presents, having a regular job and all. Not like Dave who, as the widow put it, only ran errands. Dave's temper had reached the boiling point as he watched the claim-jumper pick his way through the woods as if he didn't have a care in the world. When he stopped to pick those flowers, Dave had been in a simmer. Now he was just about ready to bust.

Sneakin', thievin' skunk. The words gushed into Dave's brain. Only woman ever interested in marrying him, and here was Jace Cutter, trying to steal her away. Pretending to urge him on, knowing full well Dave would resist like an untamed stallion. Dave tried to corral his ire. The widda was sweet on *him*. Hadn't she practically proposed to him only a couple days ago? Dave placated himself. She'd soon send Jace packing. Why, she'd take Jace's flowers and throw them out, and him after them. And none too gently either.

As Jace's horse moved easily down the slope to the widow's cabin, Dave dodged off the trail and hunkered down in a stand of pine just above. There he waited in anticipation for the widow to slam the door in Jace's face. This was it. This was when she tossed him down the steps. . . . Only she didn't. Instead, she smiled and accepted the flowers, smelling them appreciatively.

Dave stared at her. He had never seen her looking

like that before. She was right pretty in a pink-striped dress with a ribbon in her hair. Come to think on it, she looked like a girl, with her hair down in curls that-away. Why didn't she dress up like that for him, Dave wondered jealously. He craned his neck as she accepted the jar of honey and the small brown parcel. Her smile was wide as she invited Jace into the house.

"What's goin' on here?" he muttered. Well, he would just wait, no matter how long it took, Dave determined.

Leaving his horse, Dave worked his way down the slope and crouched in some prickly bushes for a better look. Through the curtained window he could see Jace just sit himself down as if he was at home.

The widda set a heaping plate of doughnuts in front of him and a big mug of coffee. The sight of all that food made Dave hungry. Doughnuts and a cup of coffee sounded mighty good.

He watched as Jace downed three, four, six doughnuts and three cups of coffee. Dave swallowed hard. He could almost taste them.

They talked all the while, though what the widda had to say to the likes of Jace Cutter, Dave couldn't rightly guess. If he had been closer, he would have known they were speaking of him.

When Jace first arrived at Angela Wright's door, he had accompanied his "Good morning, Mrs. Wright" with removing his hat and making a proper bow. He hoped Dave noted that. "I've brought you some flow-ers and a jar of honey from Penelope Holt. Also"—he presented the package—"I sharpened your scissors for you."

"Thank you, Mr. Cutter. How kind of you to come all this way just to bring me these." She blushed and glanced past him.

"Don't be looking around, Mrs. Wright," he whis-pered. "That varmint Dave Merrill followed me from the fort. Just give me a big smile and invite me in. That should get him going."

Angela's face registered surprise, then understand-ing. She seemed delighted to find that Dave was inter-ested enough to stalk Jace through the woods to her cabin. She laughed happily and stood aside for him to enter.

For the next while, Jace told her of his scheme to make Dave jealous.

"I think it's finally penetrating his thick skull that you might not sit around waiting for him. Let him know there's competition! When you see him, be po-lite, but don't go looking at him as if he were a prize. He isn't! Make him catch you."

It was Jace's first attempt at matchmaking, and he didn't even know if his advice was any good, but it didn't stop him from giving it freely.

"It's kind of you to volunteer," she said, smoothing the neat blue and white tablecloth with graceful hands.

She had a pretty smile. Come to think on it, she was a very pretty young woman.

They spent time talking about Dave, discussing his good points, which were few, and his defects, which were many. As his visit ended, Jace felt he had done much toward paving the way for his ungrateful friend.

"I believe I'll have one more doughnut, and then I'll be off. I don't want Dave to get sunstroke." They both laughed at this as they pictured Merrill squatting there under the hot sun.

She packed up the rest of the doughnuts and handed them to him as he left. She had put them into a small basket and tied the ribbon from her package of scissors around the handle.

"Thank you, ma'am." He smiled. "That red ribbon alone ought to infuriate him."

When he left, he held the basket high so Dave could get a good gander at it and the red ribbon so prominently displayed.

It was all meant to arouse Dave, and it sure did the trick. When Dave saw the basket, he drew in his breath. Jace had taken the rest of the doughnuts with him, the thievin' snake. He stared as Jace rode off, humming a tune.

In considerably bad spirits, Dave climbed out of hiding, mounted up, and rode toward the fort after Jace. He was hot, tired, and thirsty, and his skin itched from squatting in those blasted prickly bushes for the last two hours. When he thought of his so-called friend, his impulse bordered on the murderous.

Confound him! Dave went through every cuss word he could think of to describe Jace Cutter, and he knew plenty. So consumed was he with jealousy that he didn't even notice the party of Indians, almost a dozen of them, as they crept through some rocks and poured into the woods Jace and Dave were traversing.

Dave stopped at the end of a small cliff, watching Jace's horse meandering through the forest. He didn't want to get too close to him, or Jace might spot him. The Indians stopped as well, about fifty feet from Dave, looking over the same cliff, their eyes searching for white men.

Jace was already gone, his figure swallowed up in the thick trees, his horse's hooves muffled by layers of moss and rotted leaves. Dave was now alone. Dave, who saw nothing but his rival; Dave, who always bragged how he had outwitted every Injun known to man; Dave now sat on his horse within spitting distance of the war party, and he was too consumed with jealousy to be careful.

Dave finally started down the easy slope to the right, just as the Indians peeled off to the left. Neither party spotted the other.

Dave would never know how close he had come to death in those sunny woods, but even he would acknowledge that luck sometimes runs out. Today he had been fortunate. Next time he might not be.

Unaware of the danger he had avoided through no

V. S. Meszaros

skill of his own, Dave was at leisure to continue to call names down upon Jace's head.

When he arrived at the fort, that hound, Jace, was just dismounting. He still held the basket, and he was treating it as if it were glass or something.

A wave of annoyance washed over Dave anew. "Catch anything?" he snapped coldly, approaching Jace and standing there, hands on hips, eyeing the basket pointedly.

"Oh, not much." Jace grinned. "Just snared me a doughnut or two is all. I stalked 'em through the woods. They have very good hearing, you know, especially the ones with sugar on top. They tried to run away, but I grabbed them and put them into this here basket."

Dave's eyes were burning slits of anger. "I suppose you think you're funny or somethin'," he hissed.

"Some people find me amusing," Jace said significantly.

"Well, I don't. I don't find nothin' amusing about you." He pushed up to him till they were standing chest to chest. Dave stared with loathing, and Jace stared back, trying to stop himself from laughing. "What are your intentions toward the widda? You oughtn't to give a lady presents if you're not serious. You oughtn't lead her on with flowers and honey and oddities! What was in that package you brought her?" he shot out.

"What does it matter to you? You said you're not interested." Jace shrugged.

"I'm a-wonderin' what kind of low-crawlin' critter would do that kind of thing to an innocent woman," Dave said through clenched teeth.

"Ah, well, curiosity is no excuse for bad manners. Now, if you'll excuse me, the widow gave me a chore to do. I've got some doughnuts to eat. I would give you a few, but there's only six left, and the widow ordered me to eat every last one of them myself." He walked past Dave, who was still sputtering with impotent wrath.

Jace chuckled. Aside from his genuine desire to see that Angie Wright got what she apparently wanted, Jace's other motive was not so altruistic. He itched to see Dave lovelorn. It would be an interesting spectacle. Jace felt confident that Dave was already experiencing the unpleasant sensation of jealousy. It would do him a world of good. Jace's third motive was the benefit of Angie's baking. Those doughnuts were really good. It was too bad Dave couldn't have any. But the wages of braggarts were obviously not doughnuts.

The next time he went to see Angela Wright, Jace picked his own flowers. For a whole half hour he went through the fields outside the fort, carefully collecting them, aware that Dave again watched. When he got to Mrs. Wright's house, he cut some firewood, stripping off his shirt and going at it in full view of Dave, who had once again followed.

Jace knew it wouldn't take much more to break him.

He could feel the waves of anger reaching out to him every time he encountered the lean, blue-eyed ranger over the next few days.

After another visit or two he knew Dave would be ready to take matters into his own hands. He just needed a good kick in the right direction.

Jace's prediction proved true. Two more visits to the widow's house and Dave had had enough of Jace and his doughnut-eating ways. That night, Dave sat at the campfire with his friends and chewed disgustedly on his meat and beans. It wasn't bad meat and beans, but he had it every night. All summer long, in fact. Except in winter, when they just had meat—if the hunting was good. Afterward there was molasses and bread, but molasses and bread wasn't doughnuts. It wasn't apple pie either, which was what Jace had eaten to-night. He'd seen him bringing some home with him—again!

Morosely Dave studied his feet. His socks did have holes in them, as Jace had guessed, and terribly un-comfortable they were. It would be nice to have some-one darn them before the holes got so big that half his foot stuck through. He put down his plate, suddenly losing his appetite.

"Hey, Dave," Monty asked, "ain't you aimin' to fin-ish that molasses and bread?" he asked, his eyes on Dave's plate.

"Nope. I guess I'm not hungry tonight," he sighed. Monty took it up and dug right in. Dave watched as he stuffed the bread into his mouth, the syrup running down his chin. Monty wiped it away with the back of his hand.

It would sure be nice sittin' across the table—table, not the bare ground—from a pretty woman who ate proper. And he wouldn't be eating molasses either. No, sir. Pie and doughnuts would be served. The only time he ever got any pie or doughnuts was when one of the married women took pity on him and gave him some. Dave wanted pie every night.

The widow's woods were full of wild strawberries and blackberries. There were fruit trees too: apple, cherry, and peach. She was sure to be a good cook, with all that raw material at hand.

Jace sure hogged down a lot of them doughnuts. Maybe if *he* went visiting her, she'd have some made for him. If he left early the next morning, maybe he'd miss old Jace.

Later that evening the wind picked up, and Dave pulled his old woolen blanket around his shoulders. His friends were already sleeping, their snores filling the night air. It suddenly occurred to him that if all else went as it had the year before, he'd be spending the coming year with these two. That thought was enough to drive the sleep from him.

Lying on the hard-packed earthen floor, he stared up at the roof of their ten-by-twelve cabin. Through a hole he could see a few stars glimmering. He'd have to fix that hole before the rainy weather set in. He was suddenly dissatisfied with his life—a strange state for him.

The widow was right. The winters were getting colder—and longer too. Young striplings don't mind so much; it's all an adventure. But he was no kid anymore; he was a thirty-year-old man. And not much of one either. He'd never had a real home; this was just the last and the worst in a long line of shacks and cabins he'd lived in over the years. Not a stick of furniture. Just a dirt floor and a fireplace—and a hole above his head.

He thought of Angie. Jace had said he wasn't good enough for her; well, maybe he wasn't. But Jace wasn't either, if it came to that. Maybe he'd just better go see for himself—talk to her, see what was what. He sure didn't fancy spending the winter here, now that he looked about him. Nope, he sure didn't fancy it at all.

"I'll do it," he told himself. "I'll ride there tomorrow and scout out the territory before I jump in." That's what a ranger did: look everything over mighty carefully afore coming to a conclusion. He'd look over the farm and Angie and them doughnuts—particularly them doughnuts. Then he'd see. Relieved at having come to this decision, Dave turned over and slept soundly.

While Dave Merrill slept, the Cox farm some twenty miles away was being burned by the Shawnee. As they rifled through the debris for valuables, their leader, an old Miami, consulted with the spirits.

"We will attack the settlements around Fort Pitt," the old Miami decided. "The whites there are complacent. It is time they learned fear."

Bear Claw nodded in agreement. The rangers around Fort Pitt would make good sport.

Chapter Three

"**G**oin' somewhere, Dave?" Jace Cutter asked innocently as he saw Dave saddle up the next morning.

"Maybe. Maybe I'll go huntin' too. Catch me some of them doughnuts—the ones with the sugar on top," he said defiantly, challenging Jace with his blue eyes.

"I don't know. . . . They're tetchy little critters. Not as easy to catch as you'd think," Jace said meaningfully.

"Well, that sort of gives me a head start, then, don't it? 'Cause I happen to know where they live," Dave snapped.

"You won't catch many in those clothes," Jace pointed out.

"How do ya expect a man to look after he's been fightin' fifty Injuns?"

"The same way you always look. Now, if I was huntin' doughnuts, though, I'd sure put on my best clothes. Unless"—he looked Dave over carefully—"those *are* your best clothes." He said it almost pityingly, which made Dave turn red.

"I got others." He did. He had another homespun shirt just as shabby as the one he was wearing. It had never occurred to him to get spruced up for the widow. He supposed, looking down at his worn pants and shirt, that he should at least do something to mark the occasion.

"I have a shirt—" Jace began.

"And I got a shirt too—a nice one, which I was just goin' to put on," he lied. "And now"—he finished cinching his saddle—"I'm goin' to go get it." He turned his back on Jace and stalked off toward his cabin. When he got inside, he rummaged around for his other shirt. He held it up to the window to examine its condition. He could see the light of day clean through it. "This won't do," he sighed.

He went through his pockets. There was not much money, but he thought he could maybe afford to buy a shirt. When he was sure Jace had wandered off, he slipped out the door and hurried to the trading post.

"I'd like to have me a new shirt," he whispered to Ford, who ran the post.

"New shirt?" Ford asked, as if he hadn't heard right.

"That's right—a new shirt." Dave looked about

nervously in case any one of his friends might see him. "Can't ya hear me good?"

"Sure. It's just that you have one already, and it's still got some wear in it yet. Not much, but some. Should last you to winter. Never knew you to buy somethin' you don't need beforehand."

"Just give me the damned shirt!" he whispered fiercely, his face close to Ford's. What if Jace just happened to come in now? What then?

"Hey, no need to buy a new one before its time, Dave. I got one that came in just a little worn." He held up a nice blue woolen shirt.

"That's nice," Dave admired as he picked it up. Then he turned it over and pointed with his index finger. "There's a hole in the back of it."

"Yeah, just one hole. Except for that it's brand new."

"Moth hole?" he asked doubtfully.

"Bullet hole," Ford said helpfully. "But not a trace of blood."

"Bullet hole! I ain't goin' courtin' with no bullet hole in my back!" he exclaimed disgustedly, putting the shirt down.

"Wear a jacket with that, and you won't even notice," Ford argued, then stopped. "Courtin'?" he said, astounded.

"Be quiet!" Dave whispered fiercely.

Ford smiled his approval. "If that's the case, I can lend you my buckskin jacket. Only wore it a few times. Save your money," Ford offered generously.

Dave felt more friendly. "That's right kind of you. In that case, I'll take the shirt and borrow the jacket." Ford handed the things to him, and Dave tried them on. They were a good fit, and he left the store looking, he thought, quite fine. He'd rarely had anything new and never two things at one time. It was a pity Jace didn't see him as he left. Riding out of the fort, Dave looked quite handsome in his fringed jacket, new shirt, shaved, and his light hair combed neatly.

Who said Dave Merrill was no bargain? he asked himself. He sat straight in the saddle so everyone could see his fine blue shirt. *Yeah, go on and gaze upon me,* he thought as Monty and a few soldiers nudged one another as he passed, head held high. *Ain't I a sight?*

He rode through the woods, enjoying the cool breezes. He'd never really noticed before what nice country this was. The widow's cabin was built in the shelter of some rolling hills. The neatly planted fields and well-kept cabin were welcoming. He could see why she loved it here. He reined in as he saw the widow sitting on the porch with a bowl in her hand. It all made a homey, fetching picture.

Dave had been bold enough in declaring to Jace that he was going to see Mrs. Wright. Now that he was here, he was suddenly overcome with shyness.

When he saw her pretty log house with the wildflowers about it and the checked curtains at the windows, he was glad he'd bought that new shirt. From here, he could see that Angela was shelling peas. Her hair shone, and she looked lovely in a dark blue dress.

Straightening his buckskin jacket, he started toward her. Her head came up at the sound of hoof beats, but he couldn't tell at this distance whether she was pleased to see him or not. There was a rifle propped up next to her. Dave smiled at that. You could never be too careful.

"Howdy, Mrs. Wright," he said, stopping in front of her, then dismounting.

Angela rose, putting her bowl aside, then walked to the top step to greet her visitor. The porch was wide and shady, and there was a patchwork quilt airing out on a long wooden bench. Dave guessed she'd probably made it herself.

"I thought I'd come over and see how you was doin'," he began, feeling oddly tongue-tied. Then, re-membering, he grabbed his hat off his head.

"That's very kind of you, Mr. Merrill."

Mr. Merrill? His heart sank a few notches. It had such a cold, formal sound to it. But his naturally buoy-ant spirit quickly reasserted itself. Just standing there in his new clothes made his confidence soar. He didn't want anything to take her mind off the new jacket and flashy shirt.

"Ya got a real nice place here," he said, appreciating how much work had gone into keeping it up. His eyes swept it and came to rest on her. "Real nice."

"Thank you." She smiled. Dave noticed she had dim-ples. "Would you like to come in?"

Dave blushed. "Thank you, ma'am. That's right friendly of ya." She picked up her rifle and preceded him into the house. Dave stopped abruptly to let her pass, and he gave a half bow for good measure. When he got inside, he looked furtively around so she wouldn't notice his rude interest.

He was in a comfortable, long room with split-log floors that would be warm in the winter. The cabin boasted a large stone fireplace and mantel with some woman's doodads on top. At the opposite end of the room was a cooking area, with foodstuffs stored on shelves. Next to the fireplace a door stood open. Dave got a glimpse of a wooden bed and a quilt spread neatly over it. Also visible was a washstand and, of all things, a pitcher and bowl. Such comfort! Dave was awed by all the modern fixin's. He glanced quickly away and found himself looking at a vase of flowers on the table. He liked it.

"Please sit down," Angie said over her shoulder as she closed the door.

Dave sat at the table, stiff-backed, as Angie leaned her rifle in a corner. Such a neat cabin. He looked about for some place to put his battered hat. Finally he put it gently on the floor next to him.

They started to talk. At first Dave answered in monosyllables. But soon he relaxed and was talking about himself—not just his adventures as a ranger but about his childhood too. Then she was serving him some coffee and doughnuts—and they were good. Real good.

Dave ate six of them. He was going to eat more, but he didn't want to be rude.

Afterward, she showed him over her farm. It was a good place, and Dave enjoyed walking with her in the warm sun. Angie told him a little about where she had lived back east and what her family was like. Neither one of them spoke of marriage. They both skittered around the subject. Angie didn't ask why he was there, and Dave was glad for that, because he wouldn't have known what to say anyway. She was real pretty to look at, though, and Dave was proud to be walking with her.

When he left, he was in high spirits. She had been awfully interested in his stories, there was no doubt about that. And she wasn't just pretending either. She had understanding eyes—big, brown, and soft. When he thought about it, it was probably the best time he'd ever had in his life.

Just before he left, she gave him some doughnuts— with sugar on top. The kind Jace was always bragging about. And he'd be damned if he'd give Jace any of 'em.

As he rode home, Dave was already anticipating the next visit. And the next. He wondered what Jace talked about with Angie. Of course, Jace was book-learned. He had himself a whole shelf full of 'em. He was always spouting out Shakespeare and suchlike and quoting them there Greeks. Dave didn't mind that Shakespeare fella. He kinda liked him. Been known to quote him himself when the occasion warranted it. In the meantime, he'd think up some new stories. Of course, he'd have to tone them down, Angie being a lady and all.

In a daze, Dave wended his way home.

Chapter Four

Dave made a lot more visits to Angie Wright after the first time. He'd helped her with her crops, tended to the animals, and added to her store of wood. When he was finished, Angie would always have a good meal prepared for him. It was nice, real nice. Farmwork wasn't so bad. In fact, he liked it. He also liked Angie working beside him, helping him mend a fence or pick apples. Marriage no longer frightened him. Whenever he left Angie at the end of a day to go back to the fort, he was beginning to feel lonely. He didn't want to leave that nice, snug cabin and Angie's pleasant company for his cheerless little room and his two unkempt friends. There were better things to be had in life, and Dave finally realized it.

The next morning he arose with determination. He shaved and slicked down his hair. Then he got out his new duds. He was going to see Angie today on business.

Dave was feeling quite chipper. The day was pretty nigh perfect, in his opinion. The bright colors of fall sparkled vividly against the blue, blue sky. The blue was almost the color of Dave's eyes. He stopped to tie up his horse while he picked a few flowers for Angie. Jace had done it, and so Dave would.

He had on his store-bought shirt, and the world looked danged good to him. Everything was going his way, all right. He rubbed his chin reflectively. Maybe this winter he wouldn't be sleeping in no dirt-floored cabin. He grinned. He'd be sleeping in a gosh-darned bed and sitting on chairs. Maybe in a wild burst of generosity he'd even let Monty and Joe sleep in his barn in the cold weather. Dave chewed this over a bit. Maybe not. Come to think on it, he'd had enough of their company. He'd ask Angie to bake them a few pies instead, poor souls that they were. While he magnanimously debated the kind and quantity, a glimpse of color flickered at the corner of his eye.

He turned his head and saw Angie walking along the bottom of a sloping hill. Dave went all warm inside. In her hand was a basket with a wisp of ribbon tied to it. She was picking blueberries. His well-cut mouth widened into a grin. She sure was a pretty sight. For a moment he watched appreciatively as she moved gracefully to and fro. A soft breeze ruffled her curling hair and billowed her skirts.

Swish.

Dave froze. He snatched up his rifle. The flowers fell from his hand, and he dropped down in a crouch. His sharp eyes probed about him. That noise was definitely not coming from Angie. It was coming from deep in the woods. *Swish.* Prickles spiked the back of his neck. There it was again, only louder this time, and nearing the fringe of forest. Dave strained his ears to identify the sound. Whatever it was, it was coming closer.

Noiselessly Dave covered the distance to where he had seen Angie. She had moved off. The swishing noise continued, and Dave now knew for a certainty what it was: Indians! He had heard the furtive sound before, and it always brought a chill of mortal fear. He was feeling it now, and not a pretty feeling it was.

Frantically he searched for Angie. He spotted her. She was moving along the bushes that grew at the base of some ledges. Any minute and she would be in full view by that clearing!

Dave charged and threw himself up the hill as if he was scalded. Wildly he sprinted from cover to cover until he attained the small summit. Then he crawled along the jagged rim of ledge that projected out over the blueberry bushes clumped at its base. The Indians were coming fast. Through a small gash in the trees he could see about ten warriors, all on foot. For now their attention was on the ground, seeing the trail Angie had left. Soon their eyes would rise, and they would see her. Fearful that he might be too late, he scrambled among the rocks till he was directly above. He looked down on Angie.

Angie knew! From where he knelt, Dave saw that she had dropped her basket and was looking toward the woods, frozen to the spot. She looked about to run, which was the worst thing she could do.

Dave went cold, not for himself, but for Angie. They must not get her. He had to do something. He acted.

"Angie!" he whispered urgently. She looked straight up and saw his handsome face, usually so good-humored, hard with worry. "Give me your hands!" Without a second thought she lifted her arms above her head and grabbed Dave's outstretched hands. He gave her a tremendous yank, pulling her up the side of the ledge and over the rocks. She was breathing hard from fear, her fingers clutching Dave's strong ones.

"It was a good thing you were here," she confessed in a low voice, her mouth trembling with a smile of relief.

Dave wasn't relieved. Those Indians weren't going anywhere. He was all but certain they knew someone was nearabouts, and they weren't going to give up until they found them.

He couldn't stand it. Angie was watching him so trustingly, as if he could get them out of this mess and everything would be all right.

"Angie," he said quietly, drawing her close. "They're a-comin'."

Her face lost color. Turning around, she saw that the Indians were out of the woods now, still searching the ground. Soon they would find her basket and the trail of trampled grass. They'd know that she was nearby.

"If we run into the woods?" she suggested hopefully.

Dave gave his head a vigorous shake. He knew Indians. They'd get them for sure. Besides, Angie couldn't possibly outrun them. Dave could, but Angie couldn't. He looked down at her scared face. Dave could. . . .

"I'll tell ya what I'm gonna do," he told her straight out. "I'll lead them away, and—"

"No!" Her voice was agonized.

Dave's mouth firmed. "Got to! It's no use arguin'."

"Let's hide here. They won't—"

"They will. Now, you stay here. Duck down, and keep real quiet. When they find me, they won't be lookin' for anyone else."

"No, I can't!" she cried.

"Damn it, Angie, you do what I say!" he ground out fiercely. He took her stubborn little chin in one hand and tipped it upward. Then, without warning, he leaned down and kissed her hard on the mouth. He released her almost at once, as if embarrassed by his own boldness. "Now, you stay put!" he growled, shoving his rifle into her reluctant hands. "Take that, and don't leave until the Indians are outta sight, then make for the fort. My horse is hereabouts." He couldn't waste any more time talking. The Indians were getting too darned close for comfort.

Dave moved. Then he was gone. With one swift leap he was over the rocks and landing on his feet with a dull thump. Lightly he dropped down onto the soft grass below. Crouching there a moment, he studied the terrain. The safest place to go was the fort, but that was where Angie was heading, so he needed to go in the other direction. That meant a good stretch through some thinning forest. Dave had to smile grimly at his predicament. With only his 'hawk and the open forest in front of him, he didn't have a hope in hell of escaping. But that didn't stop him from trying. Dave always tried, even when the outcome was a dead certainty. For Angie, he'd do just about anything.

Dave commenced to run.

The Indians were spread around. One group was ranged out to the right, and another one was searching far off to the left. Dave ran right through the middle. At first he dodged from view. Bent down almost double, making as little noise as possible, he was able to cover a good hundred yards before one of them caught sight of him.

With a loud cry, a warrior pointed him out to the rest, and then they were all after him. He had to hope that Angie wouldn't move until he'd gone a far piece. Nothing must distract their attention from him. Dave didn't look back at her, though he longed to. That would sure enough give her away. Eyes straight ahead, Dave kept on running. The thought of saving Angie gave him strength and speed he didn't know he possessed.

Plants and rotten vegetation were crushed beneath his feet as he barreled through the forest. A sunny field beckoned to him as he cleared a ridge, and he veered away from it as if it was poison, seeking the concealing shade of some old oaks that reached down their dusky branches to hide him. Dave crashed through the undergrowth, ducking and sliding down a sudden incline that surprised him. He leaped over some low-growing hedges and headed full tilt for a maze of rocky ledges. Maybe he could lose them there. An arrow whipped past his head as he jumped from boulder to boulder, but he was already gone when it struck.

The Indians kept coming, fanning out, trying to corral him. Two of them peeled off and circled ahead, stumbling over some rotted logs in their eagerness to seize him. The first one stepped out and hurled his 'hawk at Dave's advancing figure. Dave saw it and lunged out of the way. Leaning down, he rammed his shoulder into the buck's stomach. The buck fell, gasping with pain. Dave kept running. There was still one more.

Dave's hand slashed downward and snapped off a thick, broken piece of branch. The second Indian appeared in front of him. Not slowing down a bit, his lean fingers curling around the branch, Dave raced straight at the other man. When he was almost on top of him, he jabbed the sharp point into the second Indian's neck just as he was flicking out his knife. The stick's point sank in deeply. Blood spurted out. The warrior clawed at his throat as Dave vaulted past and threw himself up the trail.

There were screams of rage as their quarry kept managing to get beyond the Indians' reach. Dave's heart was pounding from exertion and fear for self-preservation. Over the rocks he went, to dive into a sanctuary of thickets. They were coming—he could hear them. Like mad dogs nipping at his heels, they weren't about to let him get away from them.

As his pursuers smashed through the thickets, Dave was already out and sailing down the hill toward the welcoming forest. He might make it. He just might make it after all.

The darkness closed over him, and he continued his reckless death race across the soft, mossy floor. Leafy boughs were flung aside in his desperate struggle to survive. The Indians were bursting into the woods. He could hear their angry clamor as they tried to find him, confounded by their enemy's tricks.

Speed must now be sacrificed for prudence. His steps became more cautious as his concern, now, was to obliterate his tracks. Moving with extreme care and silence, Dave avoided the trees and bushes that would give sign of his passing and stepped lightly over pine needles and wads of dry leaves. He had put some distance between them. Now it behooved him to cover his tracks. Restraining his impulse to bolt through the woods, Dave made himself slow down. There were some granite outcroppings just ahead. He could see them glimmering in the sunlight that bounced off the smooth gray surfaces. He would leave no footprints in granite; he could lose his pursuers there.

Speeding up, Dave rushed through the last leafy fringes and came out into the light. He skidded to a halt, appalled. Damn! There was granite, all right, but none for him to climb. A sheer rock face of some twenty feet rose up in front of him, with nothing for him to get even a hold on. He was trapped.

Dave wheeled around, yanking breath into his burning lungs. The Indians boiled out into the light and spotted him. Shrieking victoriously, they came relentlessly on.

Dave's face toughened. They didn't have him yet.

They expected him to retreat—so he didn't. They didn't expect him to advance—so he did. Tomahawk held high and menacing, he charged, eating up the ground between them, throwing them into confusion. Some of them managed to get out of the path of the wild white man. Others couldn't. Down went a grinning Indian with a blow to the side of his head. Dave slugged another in the jaw, knocking him aside. He pushed off two others, then he was off running—back through the woods.

Furiously they gave chase. One buck managed to grab Dave by the arm, but Dave kept up the race, dragging the man along as he held doggedly on. Face smacked and bloodied by branches, the buck clung to Dave's arm until another one took a mighty leap and grabbed hold of Dave's other arm, wrestling the 'hawk from it. Still Dave kept running, his lungs gasping for breath, veins standing out on his forehead.

Another warrior reached them, then another, and another. They were all around him—all slicing at him, tearing at him, beating him, punching him with their powerful fists. Battered, bloodied, but still fighting, Dave managed to cover another ten yards before he was brought down. It took eight men to finally subdue him and another ten minutes for them to pin him to the ground while he fought their efforts to tie his wrists.

Several of them came to their feet with a few more bruises from Dave's flying fists, as he proceeded to be uncooperative. When they finally got him trussed up, it was difficult to decide who had won. The Indians were as bloodied as Dave himself.

Bear Claw, the swarthy-looking warrior who wore a triple strand of claws dancing about his neck—a testament to his prowess as a hunter—shoved the others aside to claim the victory. It was his last jab at Merrill's jaw that had made it possible for the rest to twist the final rawhide pieces around his struggling wrists. Now he staggered to Dave in a foul mood, wiping the blood from his nose.

Glaring down at Dave, Bear Claw unsteadily withdrew his skinning knife. There was only one outcome to anyone who dared injure the great Shawnee warrior, Bear Claw.

"He is mine!" Bear Claw proclaimed. Before anyone could challenge his right, he lunged and took a handful of Dave's light brown hair in his sinewy grip. Yanking Dave's head backward so that the tanned column of his throat was exposed, Bear Claw lifted his arm up to make the final plunge with his knife.

"Now, die!" Bear Claw screamed fiercely.

Angie had to press her hand against her mouth to keep from crying out as the Indians took off after Dave. Tears trembled on her eyelashes as he bravely led them away from their hiding place. He did not turn to look back. He didn't want to call attention to her presence. And this was the man Jace Cutter had said was not worth her while!

Angie's hands kept gripping the rifle. Everything inside her wanted to start shooting. She wanted to stop those savages who would try to catch Dave, torture him, and kill him. They didn't know how dear he was to her. But Angie knew that such an act would be foolhardy. One bullet against ten warriors would be useless. They would see her and kill her, and nothing would have been achieved. Dave depended upon her to be cool-headed and seek help. That's what she would do.

For a long time she lay there breathing hard, trying not to imagine what was happening farther ahead. When she was sure the warriors were gone, she made herself get up and climb down the hill. Running swiftly through the woods, she searched out Dave's horse. Next to it, a small bouquet of carefully picked flowers lay on the ground. With a cry of pain, Angie snatched them up and held them to her face. Then she tucked them into her bodice. He had been bringing them to her. Wiping away the tears with one hand, she climbed into the saddle. No time to waste now. Every minute counted if she wanted to save Dave.

It took her an hour to get to the fort. Every second was heartrending because it carried her farther and farther away from Dave. The ache inside was almost unbearable.

Angie had fallen in love with Dave two years ago, after her husband died. John was a kind man, fifteen years her senior. He had married her after her parents died, just before they came to Fort Pitt. Dave had been sweet and gentle with her at the time of her bereavement and had helped her bring in her crops that year, as well as doing many other tasks a woman couldn't do. When he had told her to think nothing of it, he had surely meant it. Although he had greeted her warmly whenever they met, and she knew he gave her long, appreciative looks when she walked away, apparently the thought of marriage never entered his carefree head.

As for her, she had taken one look at Dave—with his wild, reckless boasting, good looks, and swaggering cheerfulness—and lost her heart. For two years she had been hoping he would approach her, but he hadn't. When she could deny her love no longer, she desperately put the idea of marriage into his head. Angie dared to hope that it had finally taken root. Recently he had seemed less wild and more amenable to being tamed. But now he had been taken by the Indians, and it was all her fault. If she hadn't been dreaming around in the woods, she would have been more on her guard— and Dave wouldn't have had to risk his life for her. Guilt battled with hope during the long ride.

At last the fort came into sight. When Angie saw the guards, she shouted to them. They opened the gates, and she shot through them, jumping off the horse before it even stopped. She saw Tom Maxcy's mount tied in front of the Holt home and ran there.

Banging on the door, she collapsed against it. Tears now streamed freely down her cheeks. Penelope Holt opened it and had to catch Angie from falling through.

"Angie! What happened?" Penny cried, helping her friend to a chair. Some flowers fell to the floor, and Angie snatched them up before Penny could retrieve them.

Maxcy, who had been sitting down and drinking tea, sprang up when Angie came in. He stepped in front of the chair and took one of Angie's hands firmly in his.

"Tell me what happened," he said without preamble.

"It's Dave. He's gone! The Indians took him." Breathlessly she told him everything as concisely as possible.

"You stay here with Penny. We'll find him," he promised, squeezing her small hand. He looked at Penny, who nodded. She would take care of Angie.

"I'll tell Colonel Brent, and we'll get some men together." The next instant he was gone.

"Oh, Penny, he's been captured, I'm sure—and it's all my fault! If he hadn't been coming to visit me, none of this would have happened." Angie sobbed.

Penny held her friend and tried to calm her. Dave Merrill had laid himself open to death to save Angie. Penny felt guilty for all the unflattering thoughts she'd had of him. She should have known that when he did anything, he did it big. When it came to a choice between his life and Angie's, he unhesitatingly had chosen Angie's.

Penny patted her friend on the back with a cold hand. Was Dave Merrill even now a dead man? She feared, she very much feared, that Angie would never be Dave Merrill's wife. Perhaps, she thought with a sigh, it had always been too late.

Chapter Five

Bear Claw whipped his razor-sharp blade in the air and prepared to slice Dave Merrill's throat. A great shout from one of the warriors distracted him. Another one grabbed Bear Claw's arm to stop him.

There was a loud babble of voices as the Indians made a wonderful discovery. "It is He-Who-Cannot-Be-Caught!" one young buck cried gleefully, pointing at Dave. It was the Shawnee's name for him. Several of them recognized Merrill.

"He-Who-Cannot-Be-Caught is a ferocious fighter and has killed many of our braves. He deserves a death befitting such a powerful warrior." An old Miami nodded sagely.

"We will bring him back to the tribe. All will want to partake of the celebration of his capture. We will

56

stoke the fires and see him burn!" one buck with a scar across his face exclaimed. He touched his scar menacingly and met Dave's eyes. It was clear who had given him the trophy long ago.

"It is I who caught him!" Bear Claw insisted. "I shall kill him myself!"

"We have all helped in his capture," the old Miami said dryly. The others agreed.

"Let us take him to Timber Wolf Pass," the youngest buck suggested.

Timber Wolf Pass. Dave had heard of it. He had never met anyone who could tell him where it was, because no white man who had been taken up there had ever come down alive. Such a thing was not permitted. Once an infidel had gazed upon the sacred ancestors, he was executed, so that no enemy could ever profane the holy ones by even speaking of what he had seen.

Only the mightiest adversaries were selected to be sacrificed in the presence of the ancestors. Their strength and courage were considered meat and drink to the hungry spirits. Each offering gave them longer life and greater power, it was said.

The lightning that flashed over Timber Wolf Pass was said to come from the fire-eyed demons who watched all that went on about them. The thunder that rolled and shook the hills came from deep within the mountain's crust, where the dead ones chuckled as they dragged the unwary down with them and had one last dance of death before slaying them.

After such high jinks, others were sure to die. The mountain's boisterous spirits were hard to contain, particularly when an earthly being annoyed them. Evidently the irascible old fiends were easily annoyed.

Sometimes the old ones took the form of wolves and attacked mortals. They lived in the walls of solid rock, inspecting everyone who passed. Occasionally, capriciously, they would reach out and pull earthbound beings into the cold walls to be feasted upon later, when the moon was full. At other times they pounded up and down the pass, shouting messages of doom. So the legends went.

One old warrior, shaking with fear, had told Dave of the terrible faces that stood out on the sheer walls, and the restless, devouring eyes that ceaselessly searched for those who aroused their wrath. He had described to Dave how a whirlwind of sand had once encased him as he came with an offering to appease the spirits. Furiously the sand had flown around him, excoriating him from head to foot until his flesh was bleeding from the cutting fragments.

The fact that the eternal ones just as often punished their own kind inspired fear in even the proudest. The Indians themselves were averse to meeting their ancestors face-to-face in the event that they had inadvertently offended them in the past and that the time of retribution would then be at hand. No one knew when the ancient ones would single one out. Who knew what displeased them?

Now, one young buck, never having seen Timber Wolf Pass but eager to do so, audaciously suggested they take Dave there. The others, more knowledgeable, looked wary. It was one thing to respectfully sacrifice at a distance, but to dare to show up at the ancestors' door uninvited was inadvisable even with a sweet morsel in tow. The desire to punish Dave in the most agonizing way possible conflicted with the worry that their own fate might be worse.

Bear Claw suffered no such misgivings. He was secure in his worthiness and knew his ancestors must appreciate his great feats as a warrior. Everyone else did. The idea of taking Dave to the pass appealed to him immensely. Where else could the white man be dealt with so mercilessly?

The ancestors must be given a chance to applaud Bear Claw for his role in catching the enemy. Surely he would be handsomely rewarded.

"Come," Bear Claw announced arrogantly, "let us take him, for I wish to see our exalted ancestors' joy when they find out who I—we—have brought them to torment."

His vile eyes glittered when he looked at Dave. He licked his lips as he grinned and spoke, knowing the white man could understand him. "Maybe they will rip his arms off or throw a ball of fire into his belly and burn him to ashes!"

Deliberately Dave kept all expression from his face. He knew Bear Claw was eager to see a sign of weakness. As Dave's face remained blank, Bear Claw began to smolder, and he fingered the strands of claws at his neck.

The others didn't notice. Instead, they seemed cheered at Bear Claw's words. Feeling, perhaps, that their ancestors would be pleased with the gift and look benignly upon them for bringing Merrill, they all agreed to go.

Before they started, they stripped Dave of everything that was valuable. One took his borrowed coat, another his new shirt. Even his moccasins were taken. Only his pants were left. They were too worn out even for the Indians. When they were finished, it was time to leave.

Bear Claw, who had been waiting impatiently, took charge. He tied a cord firmly around Dave's tanned neck.

"Do not tie it so tightly," the old Miami objected.

"He is my prisoner. I will do what I want!" Bear Claw shouted.

"If you kill him before we reach Timber Wolf Pass, we will offer *you* up as a sacrifice to the ancestors for stealing their promised sport away," the Miami challenged coolly.

Bear Claw's face became mottled with anger, and he would have struck the old man if he hadn't noticed the others standing around with rigid faces, apparently agreeing with the leader. They were not about to pay for Bear Claw's disrespect. Several of them held their knives ready. Bear Claw gave in with extreme ill grace.

Since he was furious, he needed to take his anger out on someone. He chose Dave—Dave, whose bright eyes had been following the conversation closely. Bear Claw hit him in the face. It was so enjoyable, he bunched his fist and did it again.

"Let us go," the old Miami said tonelessly, loosening Dave's noose a little.

Bear Claw dropped his fist but snatched up the end of the cord. He couldn't kill Dave, but he knew of a hundred ways to make his life miserable until they reached their destination. Bear Claw intended to employ every single one.

He delighted in tripping Dave, knowing that, with his hands tied, he would inevitably fall on his knees. This Bear Claw did on the rougher, rockier terrain. He led him across sharp, gravelly patches that pierced the white man's bare soles and left red footprints on their surfaces. To further enliven things, Bear Claw sharpened a long, pointy stick and stabbed Dave's skin when he moved too slowly for his satisfaction. The sharp point broke off into Dave's flesh when he jabbed too deeply, so Bear Claw willingly carved more pointed sticks. He also stuck the points into the dirt before gouging Dave with them, laughing at the angry welts that appeared.

During the journey, the Indians gave Dave little water and no food. *Why give a dead man food?* they reasoned. On the third day, a light rain began to fall. It washed away some of the blood that had dried and caked around Dave's sores. His feet slipped on the muddy ground, and, faint from lack of food, he took a longer time to drag himself to his feet. Bear Claw rewarded him for his lack of energy by poking him even more.

Dave, who was one mass of burning lacerations, ceased to react. Bear Claw was displeased and used a long branch as a whip on Dave's shoulders and back. The old Miami reproved him, indicating the ulcerations. Of what good, he asked grimly, was a maimed sacrifice? Bear Claw sulked but was forced to give way. He made up for it by trussing up Dave so tightly at night that the rawhide dug into his flesh, almost cutting off circulation.

Dave had no chance of escape during that time, he knew. He had known he was done for when he kissed Angie good-bye. He knew it when he deliberately showed himself to the Indians. At least Angie didn't have to face this. He was glad of that, proud to have saved her. Sadly, he put her face from his mind. There was no time now to contemplate the good days, few though they were. He had to live in the here and now, if he wanted to live at all.

On that third day, Dave had a sense they were nearing Timber Wolf Pass. The Indians began to laugh less and less at Dave's torture. Their talk died away, and their faces became strained. Continually they looked up toward a tall peak about three miles away. Even from this distance, Dave could feel twinges of foreboding.

It was late afternoon when the procession of warriors halted at the foothills of an old mountain that crouched like some fallen chieftain, brooding and expectant, its face turned from the sun. On each side of the beckoning trail were dead trees with blackened branches like gnarled fingers reaching out to eagerly welcome Dave into their curving talons. On one of the branches sat a passel of big black birds. Their beady little eyes were fixed earnestly on Dave. When he looked at them, they set up a deafening jangle of crowing, as if warning him to get out of there—fast.

"I already know I'm in trouble," Dave muttered tiredly.

At the noise, the warriors stopped, looking at each other uneasily. "Bad birds talking," one said.

For a moment they stood there, undecided, wondering at whom the bad news was aimed. At last Bear Claw concluded it was aimed at Dave. Relieved, the Indians pushed Dave ahead of them. Gladly they let him go first for a change. Dave's mouth twisted bitterly. If anything waited around the corner, the Indians knew he would meet it first. The ancestors were expecting them. The ravenous forefathers were waiting with hollow stomachs for the promised treat. The mountain seemed to groan in anticipation.

"Walk with care! Walk with care!" the black birds

seemed to be crying out before flying away. This was no place even for them.

The silence wrapped around them like a chilly shroud as their feet dragged unwillingly up the slope. Everyone moved slowly, as if a great weight were attached to his legs. They followed the twisting path upward, away from the familiarity of the woods, into the eerie twilight where bygone warriors now resided. The pungent smell of death hung over the place. How many other men had climbed this path, knowing they would never come down again? How many other men's dying cries had rung out on this uncaring mountain, where their souls were snatched up to decorate the menacing sky? Dave wondered if his would soon join them. Was he destined to forever be tormented in this mountain sepulcher, pacing the ancestral halls?

Their climb halted abruptly as the group came to a giant black rock. As black as Old Scratch himself, it seemed to have bitten and clawed its way through bands of shale and stood like an implacable sentinel inspecting the visitors who dared come onto this sacred ground. Two huge gouges served as eyes, and a large horizontal crack at the bottom resembled a grimacing mouth. Water trickled from it, and lichen grew lushly around it like fleshy lips. Was it Dave's imagination, or did it seem to lean toward him, lips twitching, famished for new victims? He would be ambrosia indeed. A savory fare compared to the mere provender that other captives provided. The mossy lips seemed eager to get a taste of him. Dave leaped away. For once, the Indians did not reprimand him. They, too, felt the strangeness and were glad to pass the black face as they hurried toward the top.

We are dead, and you soon will be! The words seemed to echo through Dave's head as they continued on. The urge to run shot through him, but he was trapped. They were all pushing him forward. Dave turned his face to get one more glimpse of the black countenance before it disappeared. Was it his imagination, or was it smiling now—now that Dave was being taken up? Bear Claw gave him a rough push, and the face was gone.

The way up was barren and desolate. There was no sound, not even that of birds, to break the dense silence. Nothing seemed alive up here except the dead. No one spoke a word until they reached the pass.

At the top, a sharp wind was blowing. It cried shrilly over and among the rocks, rushing across the flat top and dashing itself against a massive wall of granite, where the noise split into a thousand other screams. It danced maddeningly in Dave's ears as the Indians came to a final halt. Then there was silence again, so sudden it was like being slammed on the head. Dave reeled.

On one side loomed a tall ebony tower, and on the other was a straight drop down. Bear Claw at once came up behind Dave. Snatching the leather cord, he yanked furiously at Dave's neck until he had dragged him to the edge of the cliff. He grabbed a handful of his prisoner's thick brown hair and shoved him forward to look down.

Some hundred feet below was a bed of bones. No, not quite all bones. One of the bodies lying on the top of the heap still had a face, so to speak. Dave could just make out the white features the wolves were gnawing at. Bear Claw saw Dave's mouth twist with revulsion, not only at the sight, but at Bear Claw's evident enjoyment. Bear Claw started laughing. The laughter echoed from the walls insanely. It scurried around them, then crawled back down his throat, where his lips clamped shut on it. He grinned at Dave as if the sound was tickling his throat.

He released Dave, and his shoulders began to shake irresistibly. Bear Claw hugely relished his enemy's shock.

"You!" He belted Dave on his bare chest, then pointed down into the ravine. "You!" he blared at him again and pointed, just in case Dave didn't understand his fate.

"You!" Dave spat back, nodding his head, the sun-streaked hair falling over his temple as he indicated where Bear Claw might end up instead.

Bear Claw swallowed the laughter and replaced his grin with a glower. He put a big hand on Dave's shoulder. His fingers tightened, and his arm began to exert pressure as he urged him toward the edge.

A sharp command came from the old Miami. Bear

Claw was forced to stop. Instead, he gave Dave a push that knocked him to the ground, then he kicked at him while he got unsteadily to his feet. The others took hold of Dave. Bear Claw was swept aside.

The place of sacrifice was ready. It was always ready. Dave had spotted it even before the bucks began to drag him forward. Four pieces of thick wood were pounded into the ground. Bits of rawhide lay scattered about from previous and reluctant tenants who no longer occupied this earth.

Right in the middle were large patches of brown, some of them fresh, where blood had drenched the dirt. By tomorrow this time, Dave's would be there as well, drying in the cold wind, liberated from his fragile veins by the application of a steel blade.

Dave stood there, his chest heaving. Once he was staked out, he knew his fate was foregone. There would be no more running. No more Indian stories to tell. No more Angie. He would be silenced forever, his bones tossed where no one would find them.

For a moment he was tempted to put up a stiff fight, one last hurrah. But practicality steadied him when he would have thumbed his nose heroically at fate. They would tie him down all the tighter if he fought. He couldn't see a way out of this, but he couldn't just give up. It was not in his nature. Perhaps he might have a chance if. . . .

Dave deliberately put on the face of a beaten man—a man who knew it was useless to rail against the gods. The Indians saw this and grunted with approval as their prisoner turned docile. It was proper that the white man recognize the strength of their ancestors and respect it.

They tied him up quickly, the old Miami sending Bear Claw to fetch wood from down below. Bear Claw seemed about to argue, but he didn't dare do so with his forebears watching. They might think he begrudged them the sacrifice.

Once Dave was bound to the stakes, spread-eagled, the Indians ignored him as befitting one they considered already dead. They got a meal together, whispering around the fire. Usually they talked loudly, boasting and swapping tales of valor. This time they were subdued, afraid to boast in the presence of those who might take offense.

They got into their blankets early, pulling their covers firmly about them—hiding—while they left Dave staked out to face the unknown, vulnerable and unable to defend himself. They camped about a hundred feet away. Whatever happened to their prisoner in the night—whatever came after him—they didn't want it to go after them by mistake.

While the Indians had eaten and gotten ready for sleep, Dave's keen eyes had studied everything within his limited range of vision. The closest and most interesting discovery he made was that the thick wooden stakes that held him down were cracked in places, and some splinters stuck out sharply. Dave considered the rawhide, and he considered the wood, and he thought maybe he could break his bonds. For now, he closed his eyes and pretended to lose consciousness.

It wasn't far from the truth. Lack of water was making him feverish. His lips were dry, and his head had acquired a permanent, tormenting throb. He was dizzy with exhaustion and light-headed from hunger. Dave could believe all of those stories about the ghosts of Timber Wolf Pass just about now. All his senses, especially his imagination, were heightened by his deteriorating physical condition.

The Indians had seen his weakness and left him alone. They were sure the Great Ones were responsible. Already they began to claim the enemy!

The Indians fell into a sleep as deep as death. Not a sound came from them. Dave waited a while longer to be sure, then slowly lifted his eyes to the blackened wall that hovered over his body. As he studied it, his skin slicked icily. There were faces. He closed his eyes to clear his head, then looked again. They were still there. More and more of them began to stand out of the walls, as if the coming night was drawing them forth from their sleep, excited to examine what their descendants had brought for their entertainment.

Dave was sure they were tilting their eyes down, grasping eagerly for a sight of him. A few rays of the setting sun still stabbed crazily at the pass, scouring out in oranges and reds the cold orbs of the night-people who would soon climb out of their stone crypts and converge on Dave.

Frigid whips of dread snapped through his body. The ground underneath him was humming with ominous life of its own. It set his nerves a-jangling. Quickly he arched his back up, as tempestuous little claws seemed to be biting at his naked flesh.

As if someone had driven a red-hot poker into him, Dave commenced to rub the rawhide up and down at a furious pace. The eyes kept springing from the stone surfaces while Dave kept scraping. Out of the corner of his eye he witnessed a curl of mist begin to creep out of the rocks. Then another came, and another. They crawled, mewling, toward him with great deliberation, seeking their object. Dave's heart was banging in his chest as he sought to avoid the sight. Soon it was around him, like a living thing. It soaked the rawhide while Dave desperately tried to sever it. It caught at his hair, turning his sweat into an icy sheet against his skin. It seemed to be taking hold of his arms, weighing them down, trying to stop him.

Exerting all his strength, Dave worked faster and faster. The mist swirled angrily around his wrists, clutching fingers holding him back, slowing him down. Hoarsely he recited some verses from the *Bible* under his breath, then muttered, "Get back! By all that's holy!" The fog fled from him, then came drifting back again unrelentingly.

Dave's eyes looked past the mist, and he stiffened in shock. The whole wall was alive with faces! They were all watching him, hating him, glittering in the dark so sharply that Dave would swear they could bite him. The skin at the back of his neck twitched convulsively. Wildly he yanked his wrists up and down, up and down, until the rawhide pieces broke loose one at a time. Only one thread held him now, but that last shred was like steel. Dave cursed under his breath and worked at it until it snapped off at last. Pushing himself up with one hand, he clawed at the cords. Angrily he jabbed at the mist, avoiding the myriad pairs of eyes that flashed down on him.

He levered himself up. He was free!

Immediately a low moaning set up from deep within the mountain itself. It started from one end and traveled to the other, back and forth. The ancestors were warning the Indians that Dave was escaping.

Dave's eyes slewed around to the Indians. Unbelievably, they were still asleep. His breath came out in feverish relief. Kicking the rawhide cords aside, he looked frantically about him, trying to focus his mind and plan.

Tentatively he took a step forward, and a rock drilled itself into his already lacerated foot. Dave cussed to himself. He needed moccasins. He needed weapons. He needed to get out of there—now.

The moon, daring to show its face at last, slung down a splash of light. Dave at once saw his things spread out on a rock not far away. They were displayed like trophies for the ancestors, like mementos at a funeral.

Dave risked a glance at the wall. The eyes watched him fixedly, grimly. The mountain swore threateningly. The mist crouched nearby, as if waiting to see which way he would go before attacking. Dave drank in the cold, noxious air. He needed moccasins and a weapon, and he'd have to go past the Indians who were guarding the path to get them.

Dave repeated a few more *Bible* passages before moving quietly toward the Indians. He grabbed his moccasins and slammed them onto his feet. The moaning turned to jabbering. Dave almost could make it out. Vile threats flew out; unspeakable filth spewed through the air. *The white man must not escape! No captive must ever escape!* The imagined words dazzled Dave.

Dave tried to still his shaking fingers as he quietly reached down and lifted a tomahawk, then gently took up his shirt and jacket. Bear Claw twitched and grimaced in his sleep. The ancestors were trying to rouse the warrior, but the mountain's strangeness weighed too heavily on mere mortals. Bear Claw slept as the white man sketched past the blanketed braves. They all slept, while the mountain raged and the white man slipped toward the path leading downward.

The mist surged after him. It clung hungrily to his back. The jabbering turned into a throbbing drumbeat. Primal anger spat from the mountain as the white man dared to leave the sacred ground alive. *He must be stopped! He shall be stopped!*

Dave slipped and skidded around the bend, leaving the camp behind. He halted only for a fraction of time to yank on his shirt and jacket, not even bothering to button them.

Now the dead ones began to climb out of the walls. Dave smothered the yell that tried to get out of his throat, as one brave materialized in front of him. Under transparent vermilion and blue paint shone the bony skull. Long, rotten teeth snarled; black holes that used to be eyes glared at him. Slatted ribs stood out dully in the moonlight. The clatter of bones as the ghost lifted his 'hawk on high rang in Dave's ears like a cacophony of wrath. Giddy with terror, Dave didn't doubt his eyes.

The warrior was from beyond the living, but that 'hawk, shining and heavy, looked real enough. Dave jumped to one side as the tomahawk flew through the air. His own 'hawk moved, slicing right through the wraith and smashing against the stone tower, showering his hand with sparks. The specter vanished, and Dave steadied himself against the tower with one hand. Immediately a warm wetness communicated itself to him. Snatching his hand away, Dave gasped when he saw that it was thickly smeared with blood. The stones were drenched with it. The mountain was giving forth the blood of its own dead. But it needed more. It needed He-Who-Cannot-Be-Caught's blood.

Dave commenced to run again. Some leaves came rustling after him like rats. Another bunch scurried across his path. He leaped over them, and they flew after him. Stones and loose shale spurted out from beneath his feet as he fled down the trail, aiming for the safety of the blessed foothills.

Almost near the gnarled black trees, almost within touching distance of the green grass outside the unholy, diseased place, Dave tripped. The wind knocked out of him temporarily, he could only lean against a granite pile, gasping for breath. He couldn't help it: he looked up at the looming mountain peak of Timber Wolf Pass.

Dave stared, unable to believe his eyes. He blinked, but the image didn't go away. There he was—a huge warrior clinging to the side of the mountain, his petrified skin almost blending with the rocky cliffs. He was staring directly at Dave. His eyes burned with foul fire as they met his. The yellow-gray smoke from them came licking down the mountain, smelling of charring bones and bearing screams of dying men. The giant was curled around the summit like a monstrous lizard. Leaning forward, his massive haunches were positioned, ready to hurl himself through the air and snatch Dave before he could get away.

Dave's blue eyes stared as the face became larger and larger, and the distance between him and them became smaller and smaller. The yellow teeth opened wide. The stench of his breath was in Dave's nostrils.

Jagged teeth snapped, inches from his face. Great, bony hands clicked as they reached out for the white man.

At the eerie sounds, a bolt of electricity shocked Dave into reacting. Turning, he scrambled down the rest of the path on all fours and didn't stop until he collapsed—alive!—against a sturdy oak tree with friendly green grass beneath it.

Dave looked toward the mountain, his chest heaving. The warrior had evaporated into the midnight air. All that remained was an earsplitting scream that shattered the darkness. It was a scream of rage. A scream from one cheated of his meal—a meal that had run away from him down the mountain.

Dave clamped his hands over his ears. When he finally took them away, there was nothing to hear but the soft chirping of crickets. He swallowed hard, then got groggily to his feet. He had to get out of there. The ancestors might or might not live in the mountain, and they might or might not be able to leave it, but the Indians could. Dave knew what he had to do. He started running and running and running. . . .

Chapter Six

By midmorning the next day Dave was still running. He dodged this way and that, zigzagging up and down the countryside, leaping over fallen trees and generally trying to confuse his adversaries. He tried every trick to confound the bucks into thinking he had simply disappeared into the maw of Timber Wolf Pass.

When he figured he'd put a good-sized distance between them, he dragged himself underneath a gnarled old elm and allowed himself to catch his breath.

Overhead, a ceiling of clouds hung low in the sky like rags of brown, unwashed clothes. Narrow pink streaks ran through them, hinting at rain. Dave wished they'd make good their threat. Some rain would go a ways in covering his tracks.

As he bent over, taking great gulps of damp air into his lungs, his eyes squirreled around, trying to gauge his chances of losing the Indians entirely. They sure wouldn't be easy to deceive.

He could only imagine the ruckus in the Indian camp when the empty sacrificial site was discovered. He'd abused their hospitality, all right. Not only had he cheated their ancestors out of a good time, but he had made all their bucks look mighty bad in front of them—Bear Claw especially. They'd be frothing at the mouth to get their distinguished guest back again. He deserved a warrior's death, and they intended to see that he got what was coming to him. It was up to Dave to see that they didn't.

Dave bit back a cuss word when he picked out, far on the horizon, tiny figures. They were not dawdling. He saw only two, but he knew there were more behind somewhere, and all of them were after him.

Dave left the trees, easing his way quickly through some marshes, then dashing for a low, broad hill tough with weeds.

Legs aching, he continued on, avoiding the dank, long grasses that would leave a distinctive path. Instead he took advantage of some dead limbs, climbing carefully over the branches, leaving no imprint of his moccasined foot. An old trapper had once told him of a river spiraling down this way. If it existed, it would be a good place to lose his pursuers, Dave figured.

Stopping for a second, Dave swiveled his head with

the alertness of an owl. His blue eyes probed about him, while his ears tried to grab on to any sound that might suggest an escape. He heard it at last: the sound of water. That trapper had been right. Dave scurried toward it like a rat in the dark. Louder and louder it became, until he found himself hanging over a boulder, looking down at heaps of rocks polished by water as it rushed by, gleaming purple under the satiny sky.

Dave lifted his head. Right across the river stretched out a crop of broken hills. The most emphatic prominence was huge, built of inconsistent layers of shale intermingled with dirt and sand. Valiant grasses clung thickly to it, and even some hard-bitten trees had grown to adulthood there.

Dave looked back over his shoulder as he scooped up water into his mouth. He knew that his head start was beginning to dwindle. He had to think of something, or he'd be hogtied and dragged back again. This time there would be no second chance.

Dave made straight for the towering cliffs. Through the water he splashed; then he was churning up rocks as he climbed out on the other side. With one last gasp he threw himself up the cliff's wall.

It was a sheer climb that had to be done on his hands and knees. On legs that were rubbery with fatigue, he made himself go up and up, crouching low so as not to be seen. Every so often he would look down. Far away, the vermilion-streaked warriors looked like so many colored leaves riffling along in the breeze.

But they weren't leaves—they were fighting men with 'hawks and knives and rifles.

At last Dave reached the top of the cliff. Almost falling, he managed to rise from his knees and stand. Weaving from weariness, he staggered over to the protection of a tree and tried to locate his enemies with eyes that were hard to focus.

Far back they had stopped, seemingly to argue. Most of them appeared to favor searching the gentle folds that rolled along the river for miles and spread out away from the mountain peak where Dave now stood. Some were heading determinedly toward it. There was one tall warrior in the lead, who was actually running at the cliffs as if a magnet were pulling him there.

It was Bear Claw. Even from this height, Dave could tell his figure from the others. It was mostly the way he elbowed everyone aside, ferociously gesticulating to the others, that gave him away.

He'd seen enough. Dave took off. He didn't slow his pace at all as he skimmed along the rim of the gorge. His only thought was to get away fast. He didn't notice the unstable ground beneath him. As he ran swiftly, his tired steps clumped down heavily, causing a wedge of ground to suddenly give way. He fell like a lump of lead right onto his side. The force of his shoulder slamming down smashed even more of the rim away. Dave snatched out for a tree and missed. Rocks, dirt, gravel, and Dave all went crashing downward to the riverbed.

Dave clawed blindly for a hold, and his fingers closed around a sharp bit of shelf. It stopped his fall, but in a second the brittle shale broke off in his bleeding fingers. His feet hit an outcropping of rock—hard. It fell apart too, but not before his trailing hand came into contact with a projecting tree root. Immediately his fist curled around it. It jarred him to a halt. For an eternity he seemed to be suspended in air, his feet dangling. Kicking desperately, he managed to find a jut of rock to latch onto. Chest heaving with exertion, he got a firmer hold on the root. For the present he was safe.

With a forearm he rubbed dirt from his eyes. When he was able to see, he located another piece of root farther up. Using his last ounce of strength, he yanked his 'hawk from his belt and sank it into the root for support. He hung on rigidly.

Secure for the time being, he leaned his hot forehead against the rocks and tried to get his breath back. His head was aching. A trickle of blood was coursing down the side of his face where his temple had struck a rock. His knee, jammed against the wall, was throbbing. Moreover, his right arm had been cut open, and he was having a hard time holding on to the handle of the 'hawk.

Blood, mingled with sweat, made it even more difficult to maintain a hold on his weapon. He knew he couldn't stay here very much longer. Even now, he could feel the shelf he was standing on begin to shift. He had to move soon.

Dave looked about for something to catch hold of, something to use to haul himself up. Clinging there like a big fly would soon catch the enemy's attention. Still, he told himself, he could do it. They weren't there yet. If only he could find something—anything—to grab hold of. Frantically his eyes probed for an answer. At last he saw his salvation. Just over his head was a thick ridge of rock. It seemed sturdy, yet thin enough to get a good grip on. Surely he could then pull himself over the top. Heartened, Dave started to loosen his hold on the root. He couldn't get shed of this place fast enough.

"I can feel the evil one's presence!" The words, guttural but prophetic, skipped eerily along the mountain crest. At first Dave thought he had imagined the words. They surely must be in his head.

"Find him!" The warning entered Dave's heart like the steely tip of an arrow. It slammed into his head like a well-placed punch. Shuffling noises followed. Stones were jiggled out of the way by soft, moccasined feet.

It was not a dream. The Indians had arrived on top.

There was no time to blast fate for not giving him a chance to act on his plan. It was useless, and Dave never indulged in useless speculation. Instead, he pushed his body as close to the indifferent rock as he could.

They were coming—and coming rapidly. From the racket they made, Dave imagined they had all arrived. After keenly listening to them for several minutes, however, he finally determined that there were only four of them. They were talking loudly, trying to guess where he had gone. Dave wondered, unhappily, how long it would take them to find him. Not long, he felt.

While he listened, Dave also craned his neck down to catch a glimpse of his other pursuers. More were out there. Soon he'd be sandwiched between them. No hope then . . . very little now.

The group came closer. Was that a rattle of beads? Or was it claws? Bear claws? Soon the familiar booming voice was heard. It was telling the others to look around the top, and they did, giving cursory glances. The men were sure Bear Claw was wrong, and the white man was elsewhere. They were annoyed at him for making them climb all this way up.

As for Bear Claw, he strode about, examining everything. Every once in a while he'd stop to sniff the air as if he were trying to smell out Dave's whereabouts. He came to the edge of the cliff where Dave was holding on. Right away, a cascade of dirt rained down on Dave's upturned face. Turning his head away, he stifled the coughs that rose in his dry throat. He scarcely breathed. Bear Claw was directly above him. Dave seemed to grow right into the rock to stay out of his vision.

Bear Claw did not look down. If he had, he would have seen Dave right between the toes of his moccasins.

"He is not here," one of the braves said daringly. "The others down below will probably find him. Come, let us try elsewhere." The men with him agreed, and

Dave heard their dragging feet as they moved away downward to search farther.

There was no other sound from above, just stone-cold silence. Dave held himself absolutely still. According to his calculations, three had left. That meant one man remained up there yet. Dave was sure Bear Claw had not descended with the others. Not only did his ears tell him, but his senses as well. That buck was there. His eager malevolence slid over Dave like a douse of creek water on a hot day. Bear Claw wanted his hide more than any adversary Dave had ever met— and he had met plenty!

Dave clung there as time stretched out unenduringly. No sound met his ears. He waited. He waited a long time. Still there was no sound. Dave was beginning to doubt his own senses. He frowned, trying to hear, even when all that filled the air was a deep, smothering silence. Dave waited five more minutes. Five more minutes, during which he could feel his 'hawk inch its way out of the root. Five more minutes while the shelf under his feet was beginning to sag alarmingly. Five more minutes with his muscles so tight, he didn't think he could squeeze out any more strength.

He had to move—now. He couldn't stay here any longer. The other warriors would soon be down below. He knew that without even trying to look. When they broke out of the trees, they would surely see him. They couldn't miss him!

Dizzyingly, Dave took a deep breath and started to

shift his weight. At once there was a scraping noise above his head. Bear Claw was up there. He had not left. He was moving. The sweat came down Dave's face in icy droplets. Exhaustedly, he tilted his head upward from whence his doom called.

There was a grunt. Bear Claw was falling to his knees on the dirt. Dave could see the strong, red fingers curl over the uneven rim. Bear Claw leaned forward impetuously. From this angle Dave could see his chin and part of his shoulder sticking out. He waited—as a man waits for the hangman to kick open the trap door—to be discovered.

But Bear Claw was still looking out, not down; out toward the woods, trying to see if Dave was among the trees. He had not seen Dave at all. Back and forth his shaggy head went, scouring the vista for a glimpse of his hated enemy, when all the time he was less than a foot away from him. An annoyed rumble shook Bear Claw's frame. Disgusted, he started to back up. He was leaving. Dave couldn't believe his luck. The red hands were lifted from the edge. Bear Claw pulled his chin back. In a short time he would be gone, and Dave could climb up and away. A small, tired grin started to curl at one corner of his mouth.

Then the pebble dropped.

A small pebble, the size of a pea, squeezed out from under Dave's foot and dropped lightly to another rock a few inches below. It was barely audible. A gentle wind blowing at the top of the cliff was louder. But to the two men, the tiny *ping* exploded into the silence like a keg of gunpowder.

Leaping frenziedly down again, Bear Claw once more looked out. His mouth was tight with anticipation as he again searched the woods. Then, as if someone took a string and pulled, his head slowly dipped downward. He looked right into Dave's face. Both men stared at each other. Bear Claw's eyes—malicious, black berries—bloated with the shock of his discovery, then gelled into the cold slyness of triumph. To have discovered his enemy here—defenseless—made his lips peel back into an exuberant smile. The sharp, yellow teeth snapped together as if he were chewing on something sweet—the sweetness of having cornered Dave all on his own. The victory was his. He had him. Once more, Dave was in his grasp. He, Bear Claw, had done it.

Bear Claw's body loomed like a black crow over the rim. He wanted to get as close to the edge as possible. He wanted Dave to feel his power and Dave's own vulnerability.

But before he captured Dave, Bear Claw wanted some sport. The irksome white man had humiliated him in front of the great ones! It was only right that Bear Claw should now make Dave a little more uncomfortable before taking him back. It was a treat long overdue. With this in mind, he got out his knife and held it up so Dave could appreciate its long edge. Leaning dangerously down, he lunged at Dave. The knife plunged perilously close to Dave's bright eyes, but he turned his face away in time. Again and again Bear Claw swiped at him, but the small shelf inches below him prevented him from succeeding. The anger, never far from the surface, bubbled up in the Indian as Dave dodged this way and that. Bear Claw leaned farther out; a deadly look glinted in his eyes. This time he would get him. Dave inched a little to one side, reading the determination there.

Both men were aware of the other warriors coming closer and closer. Soon they would be at the water's edge. Dave could feel the rawhide noose tightening around his neck already.

Bear Claw wanted one last jab at those damnable blue eyes. Bear Claw's knife moved; his mouth started working. In another instant he would alert the others by screaming out his discovery to them. At the same time, they would look up and see the great Bear Claw attacking the enemy. Bear Claw's lips split apart. He drew his breath in.

Dave acted.

His left hand loosed his hold on the root and shot upward. In a flicker, his fingers encircled the strands of bear claws around the buck's neck. Dave gave it a tremendous yank. Bear Claw was so startled by the white man's quickness, he didn't even have time to call out. Still leaning on only one hand, he lost his tenuous hold on the rim and pitched forward. Eyes wide, hands scrabbling furiously, Bear Claw went down with a tumble of rocks to the boulder-strewn riverbed below. Dave didn't look to see if he was dead. He knew that he was.

As the ledge crumbled under his feet, Dave was already swinging his 'hawk into the fresh dirt exposed by Bear Claw's hurried downward departure. Grasping the handle with both hands, he desperately wrestled his way up to the top, snatching handfuls of dense grass to pull himself over.

As he grabbed some breath, he realized he still had several strands of bear claws clinging to his shirt. He shoved them up his sleeve. No need to leave them lying around to show the Indians what had plainly happened. Let them think about it, worry about it. They were a superstitious lot.

For the last time Dave looked over the edge. The Indians were coming on. No one had noticed Bear Claw's body yet, but they soon would. Dave took off on hot feet. This time he left his enemy far behind. There was no Bear Claw to lead the way. No Bear Claw who seemed to read the devious working of the white man's mind.

Dave was miles away before someone made the discovery.

The old Miami looked at the dead warrior once so proud and arrogant.

"The ancient ones have punished him," he remarked, "for letting He-Who-Cannot-Be-Caught get away."

The others agreed.

"Shall we follow him, or shall we go back to Timber Wolf Pass?" one warrior asked unenthusiastically.

"We shall make camp and build a fire to the ancestors. If they want us to kill the white man, they will lead us to him. Otherwise, they may want to punish him themselves."

They were all relieved. None of them looked forward to going back to face the ancestors' inquisition. The old ones were capricious, as old ones often are. The Indians made the fire and begged their ancestors to allow them one more chance to vanquish the enemy.

"The old ones have spoken," the old Miami said at last as he smoked his pipe. He had conferred for several hours with the spirits. "They will give us one more chance to kill He-Who-Cannot-Be-Caught. Come, we will go north."

Chapter Seven

"Come on, Matilda, two more miles and we'll be there," the old trapper, Nash Winslow, encouraged his mule as they came within view of Fort Pitt. "We'll both put on the feed bag when we git there, old gal."

At that moment he heard a child's voice humming away. Then he saw her: a little redhead sitting on a rock halfway up the hill, her striped skirts bunched around her like flower petals. She smiled prettily, and he smiled back.

"Well, hello there, young miss. How are you today?"

She raised her hand slightly as if to wave. Nash doffed his battered old hat, giving the sun full access to his thinning gray pate. At the sight of that balding head, the little girl dropped her hand back into her lap.

"Mornin', Mr. Frontiersman," she said in a singsong

voice. Her nose crinkled up with her smile, and Nash had to grin at that. "May the Good Lord travel with you on this here beautiful day!" She spread her arms wide, while bestowing her generous blessing.

"Why, thank you, little angel!" He put his hat back on and moved along. He thought about that little girl just a-singin' away, and he laughed outright. To Matilda he confessed, "Did ya see that face all spattered with freckles? Why, that dumplin' was just as sweet as a plum tartlet!"

Not ten minutes behind Winslow came a man who would strongly disagree with Nash's opinion of the little girl. He would come to think of her as resembling more wood louse than sweet plum tartlet.

This man, a young man, was loping unsuspectingly along the woods, skinny legs bouncing up and down on either side of his horse's flanks, a stiff ponytail sticking out from underneath his tricorn hat.

His mind was drifting pleasantly back to last night, when he had drunk an acquaintance of his under the table, as it were. Actually both of them ended up under the table, but he was still able to crawl out when the festivities ended and claim victory. Smiling at the great quantities of ale he had consumed and how much he had enjoyed it, he did not see the little figure that hid in the trees. The first indication he had of her presence was when a small missile came hurtling out of nowhere and landed with a painful *whap* on his forehead.

"Jumpin' cockerels!" Andy Jackson cried, as he

slapped his hand over the injury. The next instant he had his rifle out and was moving it around in all directions to find the source of his affliction. Another rock came flying at him as he was turning his head, and he almost dropped his rifle as it struck his hand.

"May the devil take your rotten hide! Who's a-doin' that mischief?" he bellowed in a belligerent voice. When there was no response, he tried a different tactic. "I can see ya there, ya rascal!" He squinted around him craftily. "I can see ya hidin', so ya might as well come out and deal with me face to face!" The only response he got to this was a volley of small stones that rained down upon his guileless head. "Brimstone and damnation!" he swore with sulfur-laced words, then looked upward from whence the volley came. It was at that moment he perceived the small red-haired girl among the branches where she had climbed to get a better shot.

"Satan's imp!" he cried, shaking a fist up at her indignantly. "Come down here at once so's I can lay into ya!" He commenced to dismount. The girl, taking fright, immediately began scooting backward off the branch and shinnied down the trunk.

"Come back here, ya little squirt!" He dropped his rifle and picked up a branch. "You deserve a lickin' for that." For the next few minutes he chased her around the woods, brandishing his weapon. The girl, about eight years old, was quick and managed to elude him time after time. The victim, after several fruitless moments, was panting with exertion. His face was bruised from being swiped by shrubbery, and his boots were getting clogged with mud. He only got angrier. Finally he spied her colorful skirt, dived in, and caught hold of the back of her dress.

"Ha! Got ya, you handmaiden of Lucifer! What do ya mean by throwin' rocks at respectable citizens mindin' their own business on a public road?" He shook her as he'd shake a cat, by the scruff of the neck. "Answer me!"

"Just a minute!" a voice cut in like a razor. "Let go of that child!" Jace Cutter had come along with his apprentice, Riley Wiggins, in time to see the thin man shaking the poor little thing by the back of her dress, and he had become incensed. He came to where the two of them were tussling.

"My name is Andy Jackson, and I—"

"I don't give a damn who you are!" Jace interrupted angrily. "Is this your daughter?"

"My daughter?" Jackson let go of the child as if she were a burning coal. He was horrified at the thought. "This pint-sized fiend? I should say not! If I had a daughter like this—"

"Then you have no right to touch her!" Jace shouted, getting between the two.

The little girl smiled up at Jace and stuck her tongue out at Jackson.

"Did ya see that?" Jackson cried out. "Rapscallion!"

"Why did you grab her?" Jace asked, folding his arms across his chest in a threatening manner.

Jackson noticed, petulantly, that the stranger was a good two inches taller than he. "I'll tell ya why!" he exclaimed hotly, outraged by the injustice of it all. "That little scoundrel hit me with a rock—lots of 'em. See this?" He pointed to a red mark on his forehead. "This was perpetrated by her!" He glared at her.

Jace shrugged. "You can hardly see it. Probably got it wherever you got all those other scratches."

Infuriated at having his word questioned, he retorted, "I got those scratches a-chasin' this here little she-devil!"

Jace turned to the girl, then squatted down to her level. "Did you hit him with a rock, little darlin'?" he asked gently, seeing the cute button nose, dimples, and small, pointed chin. She didn't look capable of anything bad at all.

"No, sir." She opened her eyes wide and innocently. "I didn't do nothin'."

Jace stood up and gave Jackson a hard look.

"'Course she's gonna lie! What criminal don't? Why, she's been terrorizin' the men around here for weeks! Even Captain Maxcy. She let fly a good one right into his shoulder just because he was a-leanin' down and smellin' a flower. Admit it, ya villain!"

"Mind your language," Jace said severely. He looked down at the girl and asked seriously, "Did you do that to Captain Maxcy?"

"Hmm. Let me think now. What day was it?" she chirped.

"Wednesday!" Jackson spat out.

"Oh, no," she said with a buttery tongue, "I was busy on Wednesday."

"And what was ya doin' on Wednesday ya ain't doin' the rest of the week? Corn-fed little liar!" Jackson's eyes grew deadly. "Do ya know what happens to children who lie? The devil drags 'em down to hell and puts 'em on a red-hot griddle. He has a special one for little girls, 'cause they're the worst liars of all. He keeps pokin' at ya until you're done, and he won't stop until ya are. And—"

"Enough of that!" Jace intervened angrily. "Do you want to scare her?"

"She don't look scared to me," Jackson pointed out. He leaned down. "Where's your family, ya little felon? What did ya do with 'em? Ya et 'em? 'Cause when I find out if they're still alive, I'm gonna pay them a visit. And hell won't hold the both of us then!"

"I should think not!" Jace spoke to her once more. "Where's your family, honey?" Her clothes looked dirty but not worn, and she seemed well fed. For the life of him, Jace couldn't recall anyone around here who had a girl with red hair.

She turned her eyes down pathetically, and her mouth quivered. "I-I got lost," she admitted tearfully. "I was ridin' with my family in the wagon, and I fell out."

"Are ya sure they didn't push ya out?" Jackson asked skeptically.

Jace was annoyed. He stood up. "Why don't you

leave? Can't you see you're upsetting this poor, unfortunate child?"

"*I'm* upsetting *her*? That's rich meat for chawin'! That little nit has nerves of steel." At the dark look in Jace's eyes, Jackson went on, "All right, all right. I'll go, and glad to do it. You can stay and deal with that varmint." He shook a long finger at Jace. "But just wait until she ups and throws rocks at you!" He got back onto his horse. "And she will! If ever I seen the face of a convict, it's hers." When he tossed a smoldering look back at her, she smiled prettily because Jace was watching her.

Jackson dug into his arsenal of profanity as he rode off, unimpressed by the honeyed smile.

When Jackson had disappeared, Jace returned his attention to her and gave her a warm look. "My name is Jace Cutter, and this is Riley Wiggins, my apprentice." Riley gave a curt nod. "What's your name, sweetie?"

"I be Dolly Dooley." She curtsied.

Twelve-year-old Riley Wiggins viewed the girl with the same expression as had Andy Jackson. "Watch it, Jace!" he warned when Jace moved to pat her hair. "Watch them fingers of yourn. No tellin' if she'll snap 'em off. It just might be that she's tetched in the head. Some of them that were taken by the Injuns were tetched. Belike she's one of 'em. Anyway, she don't seem normal as we know it." Riley's eyes narrowed suspiciously.

"I ain't tetched, and I ain't been taken by no Injuns

neither! I'd just like to see 'em try! Fact is, I been tryin' to catch up with my family. They'll be missin' me somethin' awful. They live around here, some-where. . . ." She pointed vaguely at the trail, up into the trees, and downhill to the river. "They was trav-elin' toward—where are you headed, Mr. Jace?"

"To Fort Hardin."

"That's the place they was a-goin'!" Her face beamed. "May I travel with you? Pleeeease?" She spun the word out cajolingly.

Riley was watching her intently. "Careful, Jace. It's a trap. I can feel it, and she's springin' it. Why don't we just leave her here, where we found her? Let her family look for her, if they're so wishful to find her. Seems like they ain't tryin' very hard, with her at-tackin' people so much and everyone talkin' about it."

"Riley," he reproved. "What if the Indians get her?"

"Well, why ain't they done it yet? They're probably too scared to. Don't know what ya see in her, but she looks like an ornery little cuss to me."

Dolly slanted her brown eyes at Riley, who met them with a cool look of his own. Slowly they took each other's measure. Riley was a serious youth with a pug-nacious attitude toward females and Indians, which he bracketed as both being dangerous. He pulled his mouth down in distrust. "Yeah, I know her kind." He spoke knowledgeably. "Mean as worms. See how she shuts her lips tight? It's only to keep the lies from flyin' out of her mouth."

"Now, Riley, we can't just leave her here. You know the Good Book. We're supposed to help people in trouble," Jace pointed out.

"Even if they're the ones startin' it?"

"I can't turn my back on this little girl. We're going to take her home," Jace said determinedly.

"Ah, Jace, what ya wanna do that for?" Riley exclaimed. "Everything's goin' good for us. We got orders to fill, and once we get to Fort Hardin, we can have us a good time. Why ruin everything, just for her?" He glared at Dolly. "I just know she's takin' us down a road filled with misery. I can feel it."

"Your conscience and mine will be the clearer for helping her in her time of need."

"Ain't nothin' wrong with my conscience. I know a bad one when I sees one!" Realizing that Jace was getting ready to go, Riley sighed. Dolly grinned triumphantly. It was more than the boy could bear.

He strode to her, crossed his arms over his chest, and delivered his ultimatum. "All right. Ya won this round, ya little speckled-faced critter. But I'll be a-watchin' over Jace. Ya may or may not be what ya say ya are. Mayhap ya got a family, or mayhap ya be an orphan. I won't hold it agin ya if ya are, me bein' part orphan myself, having only one kin. Reckon ya can come along to Hardin with us, but be warned." He uncrossed his arms to hold up one finger. "Don't ya never be throwin' no rocks at me, Miss Dolly Dooley. I ain't Jace, and I'll run ya down and tan your britches—iffen ya wear 'em!

'Cause no one messes with Riley Wiggins, apprentice!"
He punctuated that with a hard nod.

"I do so wear britches! And I'm right glad ya don't
hold 'em agin me. If I wasn't in 'em, I'd show 'em to
ya!"

"Never!" Riley was horrified.

"And one thing I don't lie about is britches! But if ya
take me to my folks, I guess I won't throw any rocks at
ya at all until then," she promised. "Not that I throw
rocks," she added pensively as Jace came up.

"I'm sure you don't. Well, shall we go?"

Mutually acceptable terms having been reached,
and with weapons duly loaded, the three headed down
the trail to Fort Hardin, where Jace was to deliver a
silver wedding cup to Colonel Bryce. It was Jace's in-
tention to drop Dolly off at the fort if they didn't encounter her folks before then.

Riley abruptly stood aside for Dolly to precede
him. "You get in front of me."

"Thank you," Dolly said courteously.

"I just don't want ya doin' nothin' behind my back—
like throwin' rocks at me," he grunted. He'd prefer an
Indian sneakin' up behind him.

Dolly skipped and cantered before them, pointing
out the way and singing softly to herself.

"You're too soft, Jace," Riley told his friend grimly.
"You're lettin' her twist ya around her dirty little finger. Look at her, a-prancin' about. Seems like them

woods is old friends of hers. Thought she didn't know where her folks was?"

"She probably doesn't know, or she would have gone to them long before now." Jace shrugged, not alarmed.

"She knows," Riley predicted gloomily. "You just wait until ya try to unload the little squirt! She'll stick to you like tar. You'll never be done with her." His words had a prophetic ring to them that made even Riley himself shiver with the saying of them. He gave Dolly a narrow look.

Dolly was all amiability, now that she had gotten her way. She even seemed to take a shine to Riley despite his professions of distrust of all women.

"May I take your arm, Riley?" she asked, slipping her arm through his companionably.

"No!" He stopped abruptly. "That thar's my shootin' arm, woman!" He pointed to it proudly. "Don't be a-spoilin' it." He removed her hand. "I got to have my hands free to shoot—Injuns or otherwise. Ya never know who's a-stalkin' ya through the woods: man or beast—or woman," he added tersely. "This here arm's always gotta be ready. That's the kind of man I am." He lifted his head in a superior fashion. Dolly looked impressed and gave him room.

Riley strode through the woods. Dolly's company was unwelcome, but he feared there was worse to come—much worse.

That evening, Riley discovered to his consternation

that the small girl was able to put away vast quantities of food at a single sitting. At supper that night, she managed to get down three rashers of bacon, a couple helpings of beans, and fistfuls of bread. Moreover, she was always trying to dip her greasy little paw into his plate as well, when he wasn't looking.

Riley couldn't help commenting. After all, part of their provisions were his, and here she was, wolfing them all down and waiting for more.

"Fiend seize her. Look at that, Jace! She's et so much, her cheeks is puffed out like she's got apples stuck inside of 'em. Fie! Ain't ya got no manners? Even them freckles of yourn is stretched to the breakin' point from the strain of all that food."

Dolly grinned and stuffed in another chunk of bread. "It's so good!"

Riley turned away disgustedly and sat down with his own supper. Dolly immediately plunked herself next to him, ogling his plate. "Are you gonna eat all that?" she asked, her eyes glinting at the hot bacon.

"Yes!" Quickly his hand covered his plate, but he wasn't as quick as she was. Before he knew it, she was conveying one of his biscuits into her mouth, shoving with fingers and thumbs to get it all in.

"Ya snitched my biscuit! Did ya see that, Jace? Look how she's just a-settin' there, smackin' her lips to and fro. What kind of barbarian are ya?" he demanded of her.

"I like snitched biscuits," she confessed, grinning widely.

"Here, Riley, you can have mine." Jace held out one of his on a fork. Dolly lunged forward and snatched it. Riley was about to deliver that wallop he had so often promised, when he stopped. If he left his plate undefended, he wouldn't have anything left to eat. Hastily he ate his own dinner before Dolly could regroup and attack.

Later on, Dolly put her arms around Jace's neck and gave him a sticky kiss on his lean cheek. "You're the kindest man I ever did meet," she declared. "You're nice too, Riley." She gave him a dimpled smile.

Riley frowned.

"You see, Riley?" Jace said approvingly. "She's nice."

"Ha!" Riley mumbled, swallowing the last of his bacon. "She's only nice when she wants to be, but I ain't fooled. Her words is slathered with soft jellies and preserves! But them butter-coated lips of hers is lyin'!"

Dolly didn't seem to care what Riley's opinion of her was. She curled up that night and slept like a hibernating coon in one of Jace's blankets. Riley refused to give up one of his.

"She has my biscuit in her innards, and that's enough," he said.

This went on for four days. "I don't like it, Jace." Riley spoke to him as Dolly went on ahead. "All our food is a-goin' fast, and what do we have to show for it? Nothin'. Nothin' but a hollow, fly-specked little hawg that eats from both sides of her mouth. I can't wait until we get to Fort Hardin!"

But before they could make it there, the showdown came at last.

Jace and Riley had reached the trail branching off to Fort Hardin when little Dolly stopped.

"This is the way to go." She pointed to the right. "I can feel my family home a-callin' to me over here."

Jace shook his head. "We can't go traipsing off into the woods just because you think you can feel it, honey. We're going to Fort Hardin. I'm sure people over there know you."

Dolly lost her winsome smile.

"Uh oh," Riley said flatly. The battle of wills was about to start, and the boy had a nasty feeling who would win.

"We can't go thataway!" Her voice had a desperate edge to it.

"We have to. I have business there. Come on," he urged. "I'll tell the colonel, and he'll find your family." Jace held out his hand to her.

"You don't understand!" she cried. She grabbed his pants leg and shook it hard. "I can't go to Fort Hardin ever again! I been there already, and they threw me out! The colonel said if he ever caught me near the fort again, he'd string me up by my curly red pigtails!" She commenced to weep bitterly.

"Stands to reason," Riley observed laconically.

"That's nonsense." Jace laughed. "He won't hurt you."

Riley believed the threat to be true. The thing was, he didn't much care if someone did string her up. At least they'd be rid of her. She looked at them through teary eyes but for once found them both implacable; they'd had enough of her antics. She was going to Fort Hardin, to be strung up or not.

The sweetness in her face dried up like a creek bed in an August drought. Her soft mouth became hard and stubborn. The pretty little face became ugly with determination. Reaching down, she scooped up a handful of rocks.

"Tremblin' timberdoodles!" Riley shouted, divining her intent. "Look out, Jace!" She flung the handful at Jace and lobbed a few more at Riley for good measure.

"Why, you little ingrate," Jace said flatly, more hurt that she had turned on him than from the small stones' impact. He stood there a moment, and she hurled some larger stones at his head.

"Ouch! Damnation!" Jace rubbed his head where one sharp stone had stung him. "Little girl, your criminal days are over." He dropped his pack.

As Riley watched all this, Jace handed him his rifle. Dolly started to scramble off into the forest, and Jace went after her.

"No, Jace, no!" Riley was alarmed. "Don't be

a-followin' her!" He took up both packs and both rifles and went after his friend.

Little Dolly halted at intervals to gather more stones. When her pursuers' steps lagged, she threw more. All the time she was leading them deeper into the woods and farther away from Fort Hardin.

"Jace, stop!" Riley shouted to Jace's retreating back. "She's an ill wind that's a-blowin' us no good!" He panted hard. Jace was too far away to hear. "No good biscuit-snitcher!"

Several hundred feet ahead Jace slipped and fell into a ditch.

Dolly came prancing back. "Oh, dear." She clapped one hand to her cheek in mock concern. "Did you fall down?"

Jace's face turned angry. His mouth became grim. Climbing up the incline, he snatched at her leg, but she was already gone, tossing another rock at him. *Andy Jackson was right,* Jace fumed. *She did have the face of a convict!*

He got up and ran in earnest now. Always she remained just tantalizingly in front of him. Always he just managed to miss her. But the stones kept coming.

A lush valley lay straight ahead; Dolly seemed to be making for it. He had just cleared a low ridge when a terrified scream rent the air. It was not Dolly. She was standing on an old tree stump, waiting for him. It came from the valley below.

"Hurry!" Dolly yelled at him, jumping up and down

in agitation. "Help my sister! Hurry!" Dolly pointed
to a log cabin nestled among some trees. Jace had not
noticed it before. There was another scream for help.
Jace went barreling past her.

Riley was coming up fast. "Jace!" Riley called out.
He dropped the packs and just kept the rifles. He ran
after Jace, while Dolly scooped up some more rocks
and trotted behind. She seemed relieved, as if she had
done what she set out to do.

They all arrived at the farmhouse door just in time
to hear a man's voice boom inside. Something crashed,
like a chair being knocked over or thrown against a
wall.

"I said you're gonna marry me, and I ain't takin' no
sass from you!" the male voice snapped. "If ya won't
sign your place over to me, I'll marry ya and just take
it! But it's gonna be now!" Big feet stomped around
the floorboards as if chasing something.

"Let me go! I wouldn't marry you, ever! I know
what you did to my father! It was no accident," a girl's
voice cried raggedly. Her exhaustion and fear were
evident. There was the sound of a heavy metal pan hitting something solid. A curse followed.

Jace pulled the rifle from Riley's grip and stepped
inside the door. Riley was quiet.

What Jace saw revolted every fine feeling he had as
a gentleman. A big brute of a man, the largest Jace had
ever seen, leaned intimidatingly over a cringing figure. His shirt was stretched taut over the chunks of

muscle that played across his back. His shoulders were hulking, yet his body was rock hard. That giant figure dwarfed the room.

Rifle to his shoulder, Jace stepped into the room. He saw the girl pinned against the table's edge, the bully's arm around her as he tried to force a kiss on her. The slim girl fought, fists beating ineffectually, her red-gold hair blurring in a thick cloud around her as she shook her head to escape him.

"Stop where you are! Leave her alone!" Jace's eyes were deadly as he dropped the words down.

The man flung the girl aside and slewed around, shocked by the presence of another human being. He thought he had the girl to himself. When he saw Jace, his ugly face twisted into a grin.

"Go away, little man," he said disparagingly of Jace's six-foot frame. "This is none of your business. Go away, and I won't hurt ya."

The white-faced girl had fallen to the floor. In a small voice she pleaded almost ashamedly, "Please help me."

Fury filled Jace, seeing the position into which this blackguard had put her. Begging to be left alone in her own home. Jace's jaw clenched.

He couldn't shoot the brute because he might hurt the girl, but he had the rifle in his hand, so he used it as a club. Rushing forward, he swung it down on the bully's thick skull. It hardly made a dent, except to make the man roar with anger as the girl scuttled away to another corner.

"Prudence!" Dolly cried, and she ran to her sister. She hugged the older girl, then stood up, legs braced, guarding her.

Jace raised the rifle and brought it down again and again with raging anger on the man's shoulders and back. It brought forth one sickening crack after another but seemed to have no effect at all on the huge man. He plucked the rifle out of Jace's grip and tossed it aside. In a dark and deadly mood, Jace leaned his shoulder down and dozed into the muscular bulk of midsection, jabbing and smashing punches into that solid mountain of flesh.

Riley scooted behind the man and took up an oaken chair. Following the fighting men, Riley leaped onto the table and brought the chair down on the bully's head. It made a pleasantly hollow sound as it broke into pieces.

The man swore and slapped Riley off the table with a backhand motion, as one swatting a fly. Immediately Riley went for the frying pan Prudence Dooley had abandoned on the floor.

The brute gave Jace a powerful slam to the chest, and Jace went careening into a corner. His head ringing and eyes temporarily unable to focus, he climbed unsteadily to his feet. Dolly was there, tugging at his hand.

"Here, use this!" she cried helpfully, wrapping his numb fingers around a piece of wood. "Now go git him!" she screamed, pointing out the enemy, who was breathing hard and starting to stagger.

Riley swung the pan square into the center of the man's back. The man grunted. Riley swung it again and had the same satisfactory results.

"Good for you, Riley!" Dolly shouted approvingly.

Jace shook his head, and suddenly his eyes cleared. He saw the man turn on Riley. Jace leaped into action. Coming up behind the bully, Jace belted him across the head with the board. The man dodged and weaved while Jace swatted away.

"Why don't he fall down already?" Riley asked, perplexed. "Come on, mister, make it easy on yourself and fall down!" As if the words finally penetrated, the hulking beast flopped back, falling hard against the table's edge. But he was not down yet. Still game, he snarled at the two girls. If he could just get hold of them . . . his hands twisted into claws as he prepared to grab them.

Jace was electrified into action. He came around the side of the table, took hold of the big meat-pile's shirt-front, and punched him with such force that he fell back onto the tabletop. His weight caused the table legs to collapse, and the whole thing crashed to the floor. The bully wasn't out cold but close enough to it for Jace to yell to Dolly, "Open up the door, and stand back!"

For once, Dolly rushed to do his bidding.

He took hold of the man's feet and dragged him across the floor, then down the steps. The man grunted as his head bumped over each step. When he hit the ground outside, Jace stood over him.

"Get out of here now! And don't you ever bother these ladies again!" Jace grated.

The brute was coming out of it. He saw Jace's face above him, then started to roll sideways. His hand shot out toward Jace's legs. Jace jerked back his foot and kicked the man in the side. The man groaned.

"You heard me. Leave!" The bully backed up on all fours, then got to his feet, wiping dirt, sweat, and blood from his face. He looked at Jace Cutter, then at Riley, who was training his rifle on him. It was to Prudence Dooley he spoke, however.

"This fella ain't gonna be here forever, Prudence, but I will. I'll be back. I promise you that." His eyes were glowing with banked fire.

"Don't you threaten us, Big Bull Tuttle!" Dolly yelled from behind the others. "Prudence done got herself a man now, and if ya come back again, you'll get more of what ya got today! So you just hustle your hocks outta here!"

"You bother these ladies again, and you'll answer to the law," Jace said coolly.

"Yeah? And where's that? *I'm* the law here. I say what goes, and don't think your bein' here, pretty boy, is gonna change that. 'Cause I'll be watchin' for ya. Out there in them woods." He jerked one big thumb toward it. "I'm king, and you don't have eyes enough in your head to see me a-comin'—me and my kin." He gave a nasty smile. "You may have won today, but ya only won a few days' grace. Blood dribbled down the side of his mouth when he grinned at Jace. "Why, ya don't even count. You'll disappear one of these days. I got a feelin' about that."

He chuckled. "All you've done is make me mighty mad at Miss Dooley. And she's gonna pay for that." He started to shamble away, heading for his horse. "Yes, sir." He got onto his horse. "You're all gonna pay," he said over his shoulder. They watched silently as he headed up the hillside and disappeared into the trees.

"Ya shoulda kilt him, Jace!" Riley exclaimed excitedly.

"He's right. He'll be back." Prudence bit her lip, agreeing with Riley.

"I'll go make sure he's gone," Riley said, taking his rifle and loping up the hill to where Big Bull Tuttle had gone.

Jace turned to look at the older red-haired girl more closely. She was pretty, all right. Her face, blanched with fright, showed up her brown eyes to perfection. Her skin, unlike Dolly's, was smooth and creamy. She was about twenty, with a slim figure but enough curves to make her very interesting. The sleeve of her dress was torn at the shoulder where Bull Tuttle had taken hold of her. Her white cheeks were beginning to turn pink as Jace stared at her with admiration.

He realized this and said to Dolly, "Miss Dolly Dooley, would you do me the honor of introducing me to this young lady?"

Dolly beamed with pride. "This here is my sister, Prudence Dooley. *Miss* Prudence Dooley, spinster. Prudence, this is Jace Cutter. He is single, and he's a silversmith in search of a good woman. Reckon you're it. I told ya I'd bring ya home a husband, one way or t'other."

Prudence caught her breath and blushed furiously. "Hush now, Dolly, or Mr. Cutter might think you mean that." Dolly was about to reaffirm her statement when Prudence went on. "Thank you, Mr. Cutter, for saving my life. I'm so grateful. Usually I have my rifle with me, but I left it on the porch, and Bull—" She halted, too emotional to go on. "And I want to thank you for bringing Dolly home too. She scampered out of here about two weeks ago, saying she had a plan, and I haven't seen her since. I was afraid one of the Tuttles had gotten her. That Vole Tuttle is the worst, if you can believe that after seeing Bull. I never thought she'd go all the way to Fort Pitt." Her voice was apologetic as well.

"She was going for help, and Riley and I just happened to come along. And please, call me Jace."

They smiled at each other, and they didn't stop smiling all the way through the afternoon and supper. Even when the men did the chores, Jace was smiling as he watched Prudence moving about the place.

When the young'uns went to sleep, Jace and Prudence had a long talk by the fire. Jace determined to stay a few days and fix up what Bull Tuttle had broken, and then—why, then he'd see. He had decided, however, that Bull Tuttle was *not* going to marry Prudence Dooley.

As Jace drifted off to sleep in the hayloft, he was glad he hadn't gone to Fort Hardin. Very glad indeed. It was a lucky day when he had picked up little Dolly Dooley.

The next day, Jace and Riley carried the wooden table outside to repair. Prudence was making bread, and Dolly was sitting on the porch, peeling potatoes. She had the look of a red-haired spider as she gloated happily over the success of her machinations. She winked at Riley, and he felt entirely revolted.

"Did y'all see what happened here, Jace?" Riley asked in an undertone as Jace examined the table legs. "That thar Dolly Dooley deliberate-like threw stones at men, hopin' they'd take her home or at least run after her a-ways."

"Yes." Jace nodded. "She's a very brave young lady."

"That ain't what I meant!" Riley was annoyed that Jace would actually think he was turning a compliment. "She ain't brave. She's pesky! And she's mean and connivin' and I don't know what all. She was a-lookin' for someone to take care of Bull Tuttle for them and marry her sister to boot. Don't ya be fallin' into her trap. I couldn't abide to see ya fall victim to that fork-tongued matchmaker, Miss Dolly Dooley."

"I'm hardly a 'victim,' Riley." A smile curved Jace's mouth. "If Prudence lived at the fort, Dolly wouldn't have to find a husband for her. Prudence could have her pick if men knew about her."

"Then I say, let's take her to the fort. Any fort. But we shouldn't be a-tarryin' here, Jace. That Big Bull Tuttle knows we're here, and he's a-smolderin'. Yes sir, them big, strappin' men are known for it. No one knows why, but they are. I say we leave now. Who cares about this old table? Why, if Bull comes back, he'll just bust it over our heads again, or maybe he'll make us eat it. That's all the thanks we'll get for fixin' it."

"Prudence thinks the Tuttles killed her father. He drowned six months back."

"That's good enough for me. I say we git. There's three of them Tuttles. Big Bull is bad, but Vole is worse. He's only a few years older than me, but he likes stabbin' things, so ya'd best not show him your back. And Clip—well, he's just plumb stupid, but stupid people can be just as dangerous as smart ones. Mebbe more, 'cause ya don't rightly know what sets 'em off!"

That evening Miss Prudence came out in a new pink dress, and Riley knew his boss was sunk beneath the waves of feminine wiles. That dress sported all notion of ruffles and lace so that Jace's eyes sparked up with admiration. It was an unsportsmanlike gesture and unworthy of Miss Prudence, but she went and did it anyway.

Prudence wanted to dance, and so Jace did, just like a marionette jumping to Dolly's bidding. The girl got out a pan and wooden spoon and beat it right smartly. Jace cajoled Riley into playing his reed pipe. Jace and Prudence laughed and danced all evening. He had his hand on her back and her slender waist and her hands as they danced. He seemed to like all of it.

It didn't seem to matter that Riley intentionally played off-tune. Dolly made up for it in sheer volume and enthusiasm. She also added her considerable voice, which merely increased the racket. Still, love was apparently deaf. Jace and Prudence didn't appear to notice anything but each other. They sashayed and bowed as if they were listening to music from heaven. When it was all done, everyone retired contentedly to bed.

Everyone except Riley. "My ears hurt," he complained, disgruntled. "That Dolly Dooley sure beats a mean pan." Jace did not reply. He lay there with his eyes closed, thinking of Prudence. Riley shook his head resignedly. Jace had gone to a place where no one could talk to him. As for Riley, he was sorry they'd ever come to know the Dooleys.

The pair spent a few more days making the house more cozy for the girls and helping with the farm. Finally, reluctantly, Jace had to leave.

"You're in charge now, Riley," he said, putting his

hand on the boy's shoulder. "I know the girls are in good hands." Riley tried to look modest. "I intend to do my level best, Jace, but I still don't like you travelin' by yourself." Riley frowned. "And don't you be goin' dream-walkin' in them woods. Keep your eyes firmly about ya. Ya know what Bull Tuttle said. He and his kin might just be around, and iffen they ain't, them Injuns are sure to be."

"Don't worry about me," Jace reassured him. Riley was going to impart more words of wisdom, but Jace was concentrating on Prudence now. Her eyes were filled with tears—Dolly's too, although Riley doubted the sincerity of hers. It didn't seem possible that a little hedgehog like Dolly had any nice feelings at all.

"Please come back," Prudence sobbed.

"I certainly will!" Jace leaned forward and kissed Prudence on the lips.

Riley gasped. He kissed her again, and Prudence put her arms around his neck, hugging him warmly. How could Jace let this get so outta hand?

When they were finished kissing and whispering loving words, Jace took up his rifle. "I'll be back in four days," he promised heartily, "five at the most. We might have to gather more men together at Fort Hardin, then we're all going after the Tuttles, every man jack of us. They'll never bother you again."

All three watched as Jace marched away. At the edge of the woods he turned to wave. They all waved back. Then he disappeared.

"Pretty soon all our problems will be over," Dolly enthused.

Riley looked at Prudence.

She bit her lip. "Do you think he'll be all right, Riley?"

Riley warmed to her. "Mayhap. I'll follow him a-ways, just for a mile or two," he suggested.

Prudence looked relieved. "That's a good idea."

Riley started to move in that direction when the cows suddenly knocked the gate open and began to disperse.

"Dang blast it!" Riley swore. He ran to chase them back. By the time he persuaded the last cow back into the pasture, too much time had passed. He took his hat off his head and wiped the perspiration away. "Aw, well, he'll probably be allright," Riley told himself. "He's only two days' walk from the fort. Don't know why I worry myself so much."

Dolly sat back and put her bare feet up on the porch rail to air out her toes. She splayed them wide and flicked them about. With her hands folded across her stomach, she exhaled with relief. "Don't ya fret none, Riley. All our troubles is over. I'm just gonna laze back in the sunshine and watch my toes grow, 'cause Uncle Jace is gonna take care of us all!"

Chapter Eight

From a pocket of rocks tucked into one of the many granite shelves that clung to the side of Hadley Hill, the barrel of a rifle poked out. It was pointed toward the trail below. Someone would soon appear on that trail, and the big man behind the rifle wanted to make sure he had a good shot.

It had been several days since Bull and Jace Cutter had come to blows. Jace had won that round, but that was all Bull would allow him. Now Jace was stepping into Tuttle territory. Bull had watched, cool-eyed, as Jace left the Dooley farm that morning. He was on his way to Fort Hardin to lay his suspicions in front of the colonel. Bull knew that. He also knew that Jace Cutter was going nowhere. Except straight to hell. The thick

117

fingers played impatiently with the trigger. And he was going to send him there.

A snarl of anticipation twisted his homely features as an uncovered head came into view. The fringe of Cutter's buckskin jacket swung jauntily as the silversmith made his way through the woods.

Tuttle leaned down and took aim. It was still too far a shot. He'd wait until Cutter got closer. Bull wanted to see the look on his face when the bullet tore into him. Right now Cutter was smiling like a fool, thinking of Prudence Dooley. In a few minutes he wouldn't be thinking of anything.

A little closer. Just a little closer . . . Bull's finger tightened.

Despite the ominous warning Bull Tuttle had thrown down to Jace before his departure, Jace was not particularly worried that sunny morning. Neither Bull nor his brothers had come near the Dooley homestead since Jace had shown him what was what. He figured Bull was all bluster and was probably even now packing his shabby bags and heading for parts unknown. There had been a lot of talk about how fierce the Tuttle brothers were, but Jace reckoned that's all it had been—talk.

A speck of worry had appeared on Jace's horizon as he contemplated leaving Riley in charge at the Dooleys', but he had flicked it away. Riley could handle things. He was serious for his age, and clever. Moreover, his opinion of the human race was decidedly low, and he suspected everyone they met of either trying to cheat them or kill them. Oftentimes the lad had been right, Jace had to admit ruefully. He was confident that Riley would keep a sharp lookout for trouble, particularly when it came in the form of a Tuttle. Unlike Jace, Riley did not seem cheered that the Tuttles had not made an appearance.

"Them that bides their time is the worst," Riley had stated unequivocally.

Jace had shrugged. One of them had to stay and one go for help. Actually, Jace felt rather guilty, leaving Riley at the homestead while he took a pleasant walk to Fort Hardin. It was a beautiful day.

Jace breathed in the sweet scent of wildflowers. Their pretty, bobbing heads reminded him of Prudence Dooley. She was never far from his mind. He allowed himself to dwell appreciatively on her now: her lovely face, her slender form, her sweet ways. Jace admitted the thought of marriage had occurred to him almost from the start. It kept on occurring, and he knew he was going to ask her to marry him when he got back.

Jace chuckled to himself. He wondered what Bull Tuttle would say to that. It would infuriate him to know that he had been the means of bringing Jace and Prudence together. Jace consigned Bull to the devil. Why should he let him ruin this nice day? Jace would probably never see him again anyway.

* * *

Bull Tuttle grinned down the barrel of his rifle, and his finger began to squeeze the trigger. He stopped. Then he frowned. His big shoulders froze. His ear had picked up a noise. It might be that little runt, Riley. But, no, it was coming from up ahead. Bull Tuttle eased his finger off the trigger and leaned forward to listen and look.

His black eyes glanced at Jace, but Cutter didn't appear to hear anything. Bull's gaze went back to the trees. Something was coming, and it was starting to make noise—a whole lot of noise. Bull kept his eyes fastened on the trail. It might be a contingent of soldiers. In that case he'd be out of here quicker than scat. Bull hunkered down while Jace kept ignorantly going forward.

Then Bull saw them. His shoulders started to heave with silent laughter. It was not soldiers. Bull saw the painted faces, the war ponies, and the loaded rifles. A whole crowd of Shawnee was coming down the path. When Jace Cutter rounded that bend, he'd be looking down their throats.

Bull ducked down. It was time to get out of there. He'd leave Cutter to those redskins. Why, it was even better than killing him. Quickly backing down the steep hill, Bull took off for his camp. This was his lucky day. A nice day to pay the Dooleys a visit.

Jace, unaware of danger from either the rocks or the woods, kept on walking. It was the sight of the Shawnee war party practically in front of him that made him come up sharp, his heart flying into his throat. Without even thinking he threw his rifle to his shoulder. When the Indians looked up and saw him, he shot one of them right in his brisket. The buck's triumphant cry strangled in his throat as the blood gushed out. Enraged, the others lunged forward.

Jace Cutter was gone, haring off down the trail and out of sight. Their black hunters' eyes tried to pierce the thinning film of rifle smoke to locate their target. All moved at once, and a bottleneck formed on the narrow trail. The injured warrior's horse, a beautiful white stallion, went crazy at the smell of blood, the gunfire, and the screaming of the Indians. The high-strung animal started bucking madly. The dying Indian tumbled off and onto the ground right beneath the slashing hooves. The stallion slammed down on him, all twelve hundred pounds of raging muscle, and the last vestiges of life were crushed out of the man's chest.

Someone finally leaped off his horse and rushed to help. Four more were needed to wrench the stallion back and pull him out of the way so the other warriors could edge past.

They took off after Jace, digging their heels into the ponies' flanks and waving their 'hawks in the air. He was on foot. They were on horseback. The Indians knew it was only a matter of time before they caught up with him.

* * *

Ever since Jace had left him in charge, Riley prowled the Dooley premises, getting acquainted with the buildings, the animals, and the forests surrounding the farm. Bull hadn't returned yet—and neither had Jace. Both had him plumb worried. He stood on the porch now, chewing a straw, while he held his rifle in his hand. He took his position seriously. Jace had left him in charge, and he aimed to keep order. His sharp eyes played over the woods. Nothin'. Not a blamed thing. It should have made Riley relax, but it didn't. It made him feel like he was standin' on something real unpleasant and didn't know what it was yet.

Outside, Miss Prudence was hanging out the wash. She sure washed an awful lot. Right now, she was hanging up the dress she had worn for Jace. Jace had sure liked it on her. It had lace and ribbons enough to entangle a man so's he didn't know what he was doing. Before he could turn around and look at himself, he'd find himself wed for sure. There she was, a-pattin' it and smoothin' it out, makin' Riley plumb worried for his friend. She even wanted to wash Riley's shirt! And him only wearing it a month since its last washing. Critically, he eyed Dolly's coarse drawers hangin' on the line. Plain drawers for a plain girl. He could hear her inside the cabin, sweeping the floor.

It was right nice just standin' there on the porch with the women doing all the work. 'Course, they couldn't do it so casual-like if he weren't watchin' over them. He sighed. It was a heavy responsibility, but he was the one to do it. He wondered how them women had existed before, all alone. He felt mighty sorry for Miss Prudence. Not Dolly, though. She could take on a whole nest of Shawnee. But Miss Prudence was different.

Prudence came back to the house, smiling at Riley. "Supper will be done soon, Riley."

"Thank you, ma'am, I'll be glad to partake of it." Jace had taught him to be polite. Riley glared once more around him, then slowly went inside. The table was already laid, and Riley could smell the meat and potatoes. He swaggered over and took the chair offered to him. Dolly started to sit across from him, right in front of the window.

"Excuse me, Miss Dolly Dooley," he interrupted, "but I need ya to push your chair aside so's I can see through that winder yonder." Dolly obliged, oddly enough, and Riley had a clear view of the hilly forest. He leaned back so Miss Prudence could fill his bowl with stew.

Riley inhaled the aroma. "Smells fine, Miss Prudence," he remarked, pleased.

"Dolly made the potatoes," Prudence pointed out.

"Fine taters, Miss Dolly Dooley." Riley was generous with his praise, and he took up a spoonful of both. He munched on it happily. "You're mighty nimble at peelin' spuds. I could see that."

Just as Riley was swallowing it down, there was a

terrific shriek from the direction of the woods. He choked on his meal and let the spoon fall from his fingers. "I knew it! Them dang-blamed ruffians! I knew they'd come a-discommodin' me at my supper!" He jumped out of his chair and ran to the window. Dolly leaped from her seat to get out of the way. Miss Prudence went for the rifles. "Yep, there they are. The Tuttles! Each one of 'em uglier than the other, startin' with any one of 'em!" He turned and saw Miss Prudence starting to open the door.

"No, Miss Prudence!" he shouted. "Let me handle this!

"What are you going to do?" Prudence asked. Dolly had a rifle ready as well. One part of his mind noted this with approval. The rest of his mind was working on the problem.

"I've been gummin' on a hunch. I figger to let them believe that Jace is still here," Riley said excitedly. "You stand back, ma'am, and I'll deal with them critters. Miss Dolly Dooley, keep them guns loaded and handy."

Dolly nodded.

Riley put his rifle to his shoulder. There were three horsemen. Bull was in the lead; he came riding down the hill, big and ornery, in a shirt that fit tightly across his wide chest. Riley fired. The bullet that left Riley's gun spat into a tree trunk not five inches from Bull's leering face. He drew his horse up, startled.

"What the hell?" he shouted. The other two brothers stopped. They had not expected to be shot at.

"Bull Tuttle, I know you!" Riley screamed out the window. "I know what ya come for, and ya ain't gettin' any!"

Bull's eyes narrowed until he located the source of his annoyance. He saw the young boy's face in the window and the shiny barrel of the rifle. "Who's sayin' that?" he snapped.

"I'm a-sayin' it! Riley Wiggins, apprentice!"

"Aw, he's nothin' but a young tadpole," Clip snorted.

Vole, a few years older than Riley, was agitatedly flipping his knife in the air. He had four more where that one came from. "He can't do nothin'."

In reply, Riley handed his rifle to Dolly to reload and took up the one she held out to him. He shot again. This time it took Clip's hat off. Clip roared with rage.

"If ya don't go now, Jace Cutter is a-comin' after ya. Jace is a-settin' here—real mad—'cause you're disruptin' his pie-eatin'. Peach pie, too! Iffen it was apple, he wouldn't have minded so much, but peach?"

He hollered over his shoulder at nothing. "Now, Jace, stay back! Mind what I say!" Riley kicked over a chair, and it crashed to the wooden floor. It was meant to denote Jace's agitation. Dolly's eyes widened with amazement. "Jace!" he shouted at the top of his lungs. "Have ya gone plumb crazy? Ya just set there and eat your pie!" He turned back to Bull, who was watching him with a perplexed expression on his face. Encouraged, Riley went on. "I don't know as I can hold him, Bull Tuttle! You'd best go afore I let him loose upon ya!"

"Let him loose!" Bull invited.

"I cain't reconcile with my conscience to let him loose upon ya, even though ya are a bunch of no-good, thievin' skunks!"

Clip looked angry.

"No, Jace!" Riley yelled. "No killin'! Not in front of the women!" Then Riley spoke to Bull. "Jace says if you're gone by the time he's done scrapin' up the crust on his pie, he'll say no more." Riley breathed as if he had accomplished a great feat. "Well, have we got ourselves a deal?" he put out hopefully.

Bull lifted his rifle and shot into the cabin window. Riley ducked as the ball ripped a furrow across the tabletop. Clip's shot tore off some of the windowsill, while Vole's knife whistled past Riley's ear and clattered to the floor.

"All right, ya had your chance!" Riley called out. "Jace is plumb loco, now ya ruint his pie! Stand aside—he's gonna start shootin'." Dolly handed him another rifle.

"Let's see him," Bull drawled. "'Cause the last time I seen him, he was bein' chased by more'n ten Injuns!" He laughed.

Riley gasped. Dolly turned white. Prudence cried out in pain.

Bull heartlessly continued to rub in the salt. "Don't believe he can be in two places at one time—not unless them Injuns ripped him in twain and gave ya half!" He chuckled. His coldness galvanized Prudence to action. Before Riley knew what she was about, she stomped to the door, threw it open, and aimed her rifle.

"Ma'am!" Riley whispered hoarsely.

"Guess you'll have to settle for me after all." Bull laughed. When he saw Prudence standing there, armed and all set to fire, his face changed for the worse.

"Get off my property, Bull Tuttle! Now! I'm not marrying you, and you're not taking my land!" Her voice was throbbing with hurt at the news of Jace: handsome, considerate, gentle Jace Cutter. Her fingers tightened on the rifle.

Riley scrambled to the door on his hands and knees. Then he got up with his rifle too and stood beside her.

"That goes double for me!" he yelled.

"Okay, boys, seems I gotta knock some sense into them heads! Rip the place up!" With a whoop, they slammed their heels into their horses, urging them forward. Vole, knowing what would hurt most, headed for the clothesline of drying laundry. Knife in hand, he slashed the ribboned dress to shreds.

"My dress!" Miss Prudence cried, and she lunged forward.

"Ma'am, don't go out there!" Riley grabbed for the back of Prudence's skirt and yanked her inside the door. Riley flung it shut.

"My best dress!" she moaned, tears starting down her cheeks.

Laughing, Vole slit the clothesline, causing all of the clean laundry to fall into the mud. He walked his horse back and forth over the clothes. Then he smiled hugely at the cabin.

Clip trotted his horse through the garden, smashing to pulp the tomatoes and corn and knocking down vines of beans and peas.

Bull loosed the cows and drove them out of the pasture. They ran, frightened, into the woods. When they were done, Bull pulled his horse up by the window. Prudence stood back from it, but he could still see her.

"It's up to you, Miss Dooley. I'm gonna have this farm, and I'm gonna have you. I don't hold much store by a weddin', but you might. I'm gonna have you either way. All ya got here is that feeble little mite to help ya, and next time I won't be so nice. This is nothin' next to what I could do, and there ain't no one to stop me. So next time I come, you'd better be ready for me, 'cause there won't be any more warnings. Jace Cutter is dead," he said flatly. "Dead, ya hear me? He don't care what happens no more. It's me you're gonna marry, or no one." He turned his horse, and he and Clip started to leave. Vole walked his horse up to the window, leaned down, and peeked in.

"Boy? Boy? Where's my knife, boy?" he asked in an eerie, echoing voice. Riley's skin crawled up his spine. "I want my knife."

"Go away!" Dolly looked up over the windowsill and growled angrily at him.

His eyes narrowed when he saw what was on her face. "Freckles! Don't like freckles." His hand touched one of his knives.

"Here!" Riley threw the knife, and it whizzed past Vole's pasty face.

Vole jerked back. The colorless eyes had an evil sheen in them. He stared at Riley. "I'll remember ya, boy. I'll be lookin' for ya. Don't like boys. I'll have my knife ready for ya." Lurching forward, he scooped up his knife and placed it carefully with the others. "Ya hear, boy? I'll remember ya." Then he followed the others.

The three waited until the men were gone before they crept slowly out of the cabin.

"My dress," Prudence said brokenly as she rushed over and picked it up. It was torn beyond repair.

Dolly retrieved her bloomers. "My favorite drawers is still intact. Good thing they're tough!"

Riley saw the path the cows had made through a thick maze of bushes. "Gonna take me all evenin' to round them up." Riley swore. He looked at Prudence. There were tears in her eyes, but he figured they weren't really for her dress.

"Now, you know what a dang liar Bull is, ma'am," he declared bracingly. "I don't believe Jace is dead. I believe old Bull is just a-wishin' it. If he was alive, do ya think Bull would tell ya? Of course he wouldn't."

"You really think so?" Prudence asked pitifully. She was eager to believe him.

"I wouldn't be sayin' it if I didn't believe it to be factually true," Riley lied. "Jace would never let his-self be caught by no Injuns, especially when he knows you're dependin' on him. Why, he's probably comin' from the fort now with help. You'll see." Riley turned away and saw Dolly watching him speculatively. He scowled. He didn't like girls who were too smart.

Chapter Nine

Jace lit out of there at a dead run. Before a tomahawk could be lifted, he was no longer a target. Off he went into the woods, the undergrowth coming together again with only a whisper of sound as if closing ranks against the wild pursuers. Jace didn't look back. They were there. He could hear them.

Fast as he ran, they were coming faster. The forest floor hummed as their ponies thundered after him. Some of them, exulting in the exciting chase, sprang off their mounts and continued on foot. They were the eager ones, the ones who wanted to be in on the kill.

They were moving up on him. A nasty hiss of bullets whined past his head and walloped into the tree just in front of him, ripping off a spray of bark chips. He plowed ahead, driven by a new rush of fear.

His pace was flagging. Jace needed a place to hide, and fast. The trees were thinning out, and a clearing was in view. No good. To be caught in the open would mean certain death. He veered to the left, catching the protection of a stand of trees. It was only temporary. He stumbled over some roots as an unexpected bullet came out of nowhere, stinging his cheek. It had not come from behind. For a second he was rattled, not sure where to run. Jace risked a glance to his left and surprised a warrior on horseback. He was thrashing around, trying to maneuver about so as to cut Jace off. Three more were coming up behind him.

Jace suddenly saw it. It was that dark-as-dusk forest he had passed through on the way here. It was just up ahead. If only he could get to it in time.

A buck leaped into his path, his hideously painted face only feet away. Not checking his speed for an instant, Jace swung his 'hawk in a blur of motion. It struck its mark, and the Indian went down with a hair-raising shriek.

The forest loomed up behind some scattered boulders. Hurling himself over them, Jace crashed into a deep thicket and came out the other side. Rolling to his feet, he was up and running again, as branches whipped and tore at him.

Still the warriors came on, not a bit daunted. They kept circling around, getting closer and closer. Jace's scalp crawled with fear as they screamed to one another, pointing him out, as he tried to elude first one group, then another. He streaked for a dark tangle of toppled trees and dense growth and plunged in. Thick roots stretched before him, grabbing at his pants and tripping him up. He fell to his knees and stayed there as a riot of bullets pelted into the exact spot where he had disappeared. Cries of triumph turned to frustration as their prey vanished from view.

His heart pummeled his rib cage as he scooted about on all fours, trying to get away and not be seen at the same time. There were shouts back and forth as each brave caught a glimpse of him. Smashing down broken branches and bushes, he scuttled deeper into the morass until even he couldn't see much of anything. Their cries, which had been gusty at first, grew gradually fainter as he covered ground quickly. Crouching, he tore up distance, trying to get as far away from his enemies as possible.

Finally he could go no farther. His lungs were about to burst, and his legs felt like iron. He collapsed against a tree to catch his wheezing breath and take stock of the situation. Pulse hammering, sweat standing out on his face, Jace tried to quiet his throbbing, painful body enough to listen to outside noises. Only silence met his ears. He'd lost them. Or had he?

Jace reloaded his rifle. He took a nervous swig from his canteen and pricked up his ears. The silence was soothing, but he couldn't help wondering where the

Indians had gone. After a short rest he began to make his way more cautiously, stopping to listen every few yards.

For the first time he began to notice that the sun was shining. It gently dappled the mossy floor. A soft breeze played through the bushes and brought the sweet smell of warm grass with it.

A nice day to die. Jace shook the thought out of his head. He didn't want to die today. He wanted to go back. He wanted to see Prudence again. He wanted to live.

Abruptly he halted. The scent of warm grass came to him again. Grass. That meant he must be coming to a clearing. Everything else in the dark here smelled dank, not clean and fresh.

Jace got to the edge of the forest and knelt down. He saw that the wooded expanse he was in was just one of many that dotted the massive grassland. He'd have to go a couple hundred yards to get to safety again. The next patch of woods seemed a lot smaller. Jace cursed to himself. It had to be attempted.

Hovering for a moment in the friendly shade, he scanned the area once more. Nothing moved. Everything seemed peaceful. He'd risk it. Jace stepped out into the light. Immediately there was a loud howl. They had seen him. They had been waiting.

He shot out across the wide band of sun-bright grasslands in a dead heat. Halfway across, a rifle exploded, and a second ball whined past him. Far off to his right, four horsemen heaved out of the thickets. The ponies were galloping hard, hooves grinding up the earth. They came right at him, gaining on him. Cut him off or run him down—the Shawnee didn't seem to care which.

A bullet pinged by, just as he switched directions, and he headed straight for a clustering of rocks that lay halfway to the next island of forest. Behind him a warrior yelled, and two more riders came at him slant-wise, piling up the pressure.

He experienced a grim sort of pleasure as he began to outdistance them. Even their horses began to lag. One warrior curved to his right. Jace snapped his head to look left. Another few were heading to that side. Jace almost stumbled as he read these signs: they weren't trying to run him down now, they were trying to turn him, like a passel of chickens, in the direction they wanted him to go. Jace tried to veer to the left, but immediately a horseman was there, rifle up. He was forced to keep running—straight ahead. Soon, very soon, he saw why he was being driven here. Fear jolted through him.

What he thought was just a welcome land swell ahead turned out to be a huge, eroded groove that wickedly slashed across the middle of the entire meadow. It was impossible to avoid. Jace's eyes grew wider and wider as his feet raced him nearer and nearer. He couldn't even tell how wide it was. He couldn't even guess if he could clear it. The closer he got to it, the wider it yawned.

Even though he didn't know if he could jump it, he picked up speed. He would need it to make that impossible leap. A leap that was seeming more impossible the closer he came.

"Hell," he muttered, his heart crawling up into his throat. He'd have to try it. He had to. The Indians wouldn't let him back down. They kept crowding closer behind him. If he didn't try to clear that gash, they knew they had him. If he tried and he didn't make it . . .

His feet pummeled heavily into the ground, and the monstrous opening suddenly was there right beneath him. Jace gasped. It was too wide. Fifteen feet of gaping space was coming at him—fifteen feet of nothingness.

He only had time to swing his rifle over his shoulder by its strap as he picked up speed and held his breath. Then his jolting steps carried him right to the gorge's rim. With no chance in hell, he hurtled off into space.

He cannonballed across the deep chasm and crashed into the opposite wall just a few feet short of the top. Dirt flying and feet kicking into the earth, Jace determinedly clawed his way to the broken rim; then, with his last breath and a frightened, over-the-shoulder look at the canyon floor below, he flung himself onto flat ground. The sight of the bottomless void made his stomach lurch. His body shook crazily as he pressed his face into the grass with relief. He was safe—for now.

He hugged the ground and almost smiled with disbelief at his good luck. But he wasn't out of it yet. For now he was only safe enough to raise his head and watch the Indians give chase. At the last moment they had jerked their horses away from the rim. Not one would risk the jump. Instead they raised their rifles in a furor. A hot barrage of lead balls slammed into the ground around Jace. When he didn't die, they shook their angry fists at him and were already busy searching for a way across the gaping groove.

Jace rose shakily to a crouch and streaked off for those boulders. Once inside their shelter, he checked his rifle with trembling hands. The hungry wolves wanted to chew off a big hunk of his hide, all right. There they stood in plain sight, feeling hugely confident, darting around the rim, snarling threats. The impulse to give them something to snarl about was overwhelming.

He brought up his gun and honed in on the man nearest him—a particularly hateful buck who kept pointing to Jace and grinning. He stilled his hands as he took aim and fired. Blood appeared on the buck's arm. After his first shocked stare, his lips moved in silent rage as his brutal glare traveled across the hot expanse straight at Cutter's heart.

The man slipped off his pony and lost himself in

the waist-high grasses. Alarmed, Jace knew it was time to git. That buck was coming for him.

Bent low, he made a beeline for the next island of trees. When he reached it, his heart squeezed in his chest. It wasn't a forest, as he'd thought, it was only a wispy fringe of willows lining a ravine. Even a coon couldn't hide in there. At the base was a fast-running stream. Jace had no time and no choice. He dropped down.

At the bottom he headed downstream—away from the Shawnee, he calculated. The water was shallow and cold. Jace had made a poor choice with no time to remedy it. He had to keep going. Things got worse. The walls loomed steeper and steeper around him, making any thought of climbing out of there impossible. He was losing his advantage, and the weakness of his position was mounting.

Jace splashed across the shallow river to the other shore. Things might be better there. Dodging behind some mossy granite, he stopped to get his bearings and hastily reload. The sound of rushing water engulfed him. There was no sign of his enemy. He just had to take a rest. Jace leaned his head against the rock and closed his eyes tiredly. He marveled that he was still alive, but that jump had cost him. His knee was giving him grief, starting to swell painfully. He didn't need any handicap. It would take only one blunder to end his life. Jace had the dreadful feeling that he had already made one—in fact, several.

For comfort, he reached down to his belt to feel his

knife and 'hawk. At least he hadn't lost them in that wild leap. It was little enough for which to be grateful.

Dashing sweat from his forehead, he looked down his trail but saw nothing, only the silent, forested cliffs and sluggish waters. Worry gnawed at him. He did not flatter himself that he had lost them so easily. The last man in the world he would underestimate was a Shawnee tracker goaded by revenge. The man he had wounded did not strike him as one who forgave easily. He'd be back. He wouldn't let Cutter slip through his fingers a second time.

"Damn!" Cutter swore. He wished he could have killed him when he had the chance. With stiff fingers he flipped his hair out of the way. No time to rest. He urged his tired body to keep moving.

He was forced to advance down the river, where he didn't want to go. Silently he crept out from behind the rocks. He took one step forward, then halted. There was a slight sloshing noise. A scrape on stone. Someone was coming. They hadn't found him, but they would. Almost hypnotically, his eyes were drawn to the shoreline, where the smooth-coated sheen of a pony could be seen. Of the rider, Jace could see nothing. The willows hung over the water, obliterating rider and horse. Only the hooves, gently stirring eddies of water, were visible.

Cutter's face hardened with determination. Taking a firm hold of his rifle, he straightened his drooping shoulders and stepped out boldly to meet the enemy.

The rider seemed in no hurry. The horse came

slowly, sedately, as if the rider did not anticipate meeting anyone, certainly not Jace Cutter. Onward he came, swerving this way, then that, the horseman apparently in no hurry. Or maybe he was hurt. The idea came to him in a flash. Jace watched the horse taking its sweet, old time. Behind him was—nothing. No one else followed. Whoever was here, was here alone.

Jace eyed the horse with savage desperation. One rider alone—surely Jace could take him! Even if he risked a shot, one shot, he could snatch the pony and get the hell out of there. The more Jace ran it through his mind, the better and better it sounded. Hedging his bet on nerve alone, Jace decided to risk it all.

Rifle snug against his shoulder, he trained it where the rider would appear among the willows. At this distance he couldn't miss. Hope began to trickle through him as he contemplated his plan. He waited, body taut. The pony stepped delicately around a branch and entered the shallows, coming into clear view.

Jace's jaw dropped: the horse was riderless. It came toward Jace and shook nervously. That's what warned him. He darted to one side, just as a bullet whipped past his face. It was a trap. A trap to get him into the open. And it had succeeded.

Spinning around, he aimed at the puff of smoke from the woods and fired. Then he plowed into the water, swiping his hand at the pony's rein. There was still a slender chance. The horse shied and backed off. Jace reached again.

"Come on, boy! Come on!" The tenseness in Jace's voice frightened the animal. Someone whistled. The pony turned and trotted off.

Jace bit off an oath as his last chance of escape ran downriver. He made an impetuous move forward as if to run down the beast.

Instantly five riders appeared out of nowhere. Two came from upriver; three came from down. While Jace stood there an indecisive second, they came at him. There was no place to go, and his rifle was useless. In one hell of a fix now, he rushed to reload, knowing that that wouldn't be enough. One bullet would not take care of his problem. A lead ball struck his rifle near his hand, stinging the gun out of his fingers. It flew into the water.

With his left hand he whipped out his knife. In his right he gripped his 'hawk. His eyes glittered with the fierceness of a cornered animal who is prepared to fight to the death. There was no place to take cover, and running was useless. Jace stood in the shallows, legs braced firmly apart, and waited for the warriors to come to him.

Hoofbeats drummed. His face pulled tight as he stood ready in the afternoon heat. They came at him through the current, riding abreast. Suddenly and startlingly, they pulled to a halt . . . and waited.

They stared at him. He stared back. Seconds pulsed by. They didn't attack. Maybe they meant to rattle his nerves first? If that was their intent, it was working.

Fear made sweat stand out on Jace's forehead. He wiped it away quickly.

Then he heard a sharp voice high up above his head. Risking a glance in that direction, Jace recognized at the top of the ravine, his bloodied arm now bound, the buck he had shot. He was the leader.

Jace looked him in the eye and snapped defiantly, "I should have killed you when I had you under my gun!" Inside, his heart was slamming against his ribs like a bird in a cage. Another mistake he'd made. They just kept piling up.

The buck looked down at Jace with an expression so irate, Jace had the feeling he'd like to tear him apart and eat him, bones and all. But the buck could wait a while yet. He had the upper hand. There was much satisfaction to be gotten out of torturing Jace before dealing the final death blow. If there was one thing Indians enjoyed, it was prolonging the death of an enemy.

The buck smiled. Cold fear blew down the back of Jace's neck. Grimly satisfied with the whole situation, the warrior raised his feathered war lance and barked out an order.

One of the riders let out a piercing yell and jumped his horse at Cutter, roiling the water as he came. He hung low on the horse's neck as he raised his war club for a stunning blow. Jace planted his feet squarely and pulled back his 'hawk to strike. The warrior swooped down and smacked it from his grip as he thundered past, splashing a path of river water in his wake. He slowed his pony and joined the others. They all hooted and jeered at Cutter's stupidity.

Jace couldn't believe it: first his gun and now his 'hawk. All he had left was his knife. He looked down at it in his hand. It seemed much too small a weapon with which to save himself from all these Indians, but it was all he had. With a sick feeling in his stomach, his hands tightened upon the handle. His eyes lifted to where the warriors sat mounted, watching him with evident relish.

"Come on, you red devils," he muttered. "If you want me, come and get me. I'll take at least one of you along with me." Deliberately, his eyes sought out the leader. "Preferably you."

The leader saw the white man eyeing him in an un- friendly way. He seemed to know his thoughts even though he couldn't hear his speech.

Lazily he gave another command, then sat back to watch. As another buck drummed his heels into his pony's sides, cheers filled the air, and the ugly echoes dashed against the cliffs. Here was entertainment! Bare legs wrapped around the horse's middle, the second man leaned sideways as he shot past Jace. His 'hawk sliced at Cutter's head. Jace ducked away. Instead of cleaving his skull, the blade whooshed past his ear. Even as the warrior reined in sharply, angry at being cheated, another came charging up to take his place.

Harried, Jace swung around to meet him. This buck

came at him weaponless. His horse was his weapon. With a shout, he ran the pony directly at Cutter. Jace scurried to one side; the horse followed. Jace stumbled to avoid being trampled. The Indian pulled at the reins, and the animal's shoulder rammed into Jace. Slipping on the uneven river bottom, Jace went down hard. A groan was torn out of him as he fought his way up to a standing position once more.

Each confrontation was leaving him more badly off. His arm was wrenched agonizingly, and he felt as if someone had gut-punched him. He wiped his wet hair from his eyes with a hand that moved more slowly than before.

The wounded Indian was quick to notice. A smile spread across his face. Thirty yards away, the buck who had knocked him down turned, annoyed to see Cutter still standing, the knife still in his hand. The leader's voice boomed out, stopping him.

It was time for someone else to have a turn.

Another warrior's name was called out. There was a sudden change in the air. The Indians whispered among themselves as the man haughtily pulled his horse from the line of warriors. He walked ahead and stopped, as if allowing the others time to fully admire him.

Jace knew he was in trouble. A disdainful smile was on the brave's face as he contemplated his comrades' pitiful attempts to rout the enemy. Such an enemy was paltry. He would demonstrate to them how to dispatch him.

He looked long and hard at Jace with eyes that clearly conveyed that he didn't like what he was looking at. For a full minute he watched, remaining perfectly still. It was an intimidating gesture, as it was meant to be. Jace could feel the uneasiness oozing into his very bones.

This man displayed no anger as the others had. It was all pride, the pride of one flaunting his reputation. His arrogant head was tilted, the handsome jaw lifted impudently. All about him was calm hauteur. He was proud of his looks and proud of his cunning. It showed in every move. He would take care of the puny white man. He would show the others how little there was to it, at the same time evincing his greatness.

When the others had admired to their fill, Preening Bird, as he was called, was ready. With seeming effortlessness he slipped from the pony's back. He did not need the horse. A ripple of appreciation went through the spectators as Preening Bird reached for his war club. Jace's muscles tightened. A war club against his measly knife. No need to guess the outcome of this. He rubbed the back of his hand against his eyes to clear his vision. It did not help.

The bucks grew quiet for this, the last showdown. Jace understood, and he stilled. This man, then, had the honor of delivering the final coup de grace. Preening Bird, the slayer.

Preening Bird started to walk toward Jace. He didn't hurry but walked slowly, his hips swaying with a confident swagger. Preening Bird, at least, had no doubt of the outcome.

Jace backed up. A light of amusement flashed in the warrior's eyes as he saw this evidence of the white man's cowardice. With each step he beat his war club into the palm of his other hand. The persistent throb of it tightened Jace's nerves to the breaking point. Jace's breath came more heavily as he backed up even more, holding his knife ready. Preening Bird's black eyes locked with Jace's, and Jace couldn't look away from their mesmerizing intensity.

At last Jace broke the contact. He flexed his knees, holding the knife lightly.

The buck's walk turned into a jog, then an all-out run, as he came at him ferociously. He was on Jace now. Raising his war club high, he let out an ear-piercing scream filled with virulence. Jace lunged at him with his knife. As Preening Bird lightly sidestepped, something hit Jace on the skull from behind. It knocked the stuffing out of him. Color burst in his head; his shoulders bunched too late in defense as his legs buckled. Unable to believe what had happened, he slipped to his knees in the shallow, icy waters. His blurred eyes looked down helplessly at the current that swirled around him, red with his own blood.

While Preening Bird had kept him occupied, someone had come and walloped him from behind. His hands empty, Jace touched his head gently. It ran with blood.

Preening Bird stood watching Jace laughingly, while the man behind him sniggered. Jace groped about for the knife. It took him a long time to find it. The Indians let him, amused by his attempts. Jace picked it up and waved it at Preening Bird. Preening Bird kicked it out of his hands. He made a sound of contempt. It had been too easy.

Jace was losing all strength. The world was painfully turning to darkness on him. He fought to stay conscious. He couldn't afford to collapse now.

Another order was barked from the wounded warrior on top. At once Jace found himself facedown in the water. With air cut off to his lungs, he began to beat ineffectually about in the river. They held him down until he stopped fighting, stopped moving, and damn near stopped breathing. Then they lifted him out and hauled him to his feet. Properly subdued, he was dragged to shore. Coughing up muddy water, he felt as weak as a baby.

"Dirty fighters," he rasped out. "Cheats!" It came out as a husky whisper. The Indians ignored him. As he lost consciousness, he was tossed over a horse's back. There was still some play left in him. They still had a use for him.

Chapter Ten

Jace heard a rattling, like pots clanging together. It roused him from his troubled sleep. Good old Riley—he must be putting on some tea for breakfast. He could sure use something hot inside him. Jace shivered, only half-awake. Too bad the kid didn't throw another log onto the fire while he was at it. It was so damned cold. His feet were numb, and his face felt icy. He'd have to do it himself.

Jace turned his head a little, and instantly his skull exploded into a hundred lights. Needles of pain stabbed like bayonets behind his eyelids and the back of his head. A whimper was forced out of his lips. He fell back against something rough.

His jaw clamped tightly while he waited for the pain to subside. It finally eased up a little. Groggily, he tried

148

to remember what had happened, but all he could focus on was taking care of that fire—now. Jace attempted to push himself up, but he couldn't. Something was holding him down.

He tried to call out to Riley, but only a dry whisper came out of his throat. Using every bit of his strength, Jace managed to raise his leaden eyelids and look around him. Riley wasn't there. Neither was his snug cabin. Instead, Jace looked down stupidly at his trussed-up body. He felt the strong cords that bound him to an old oak. The dying campfire, a few feet away, sent forth acrid wisps of light that showed the dark shapes of the Shawnee who slept warmly in their blankets.

Jace wasn't at home. He was the Shawnees' prisoner. The explosive fall down to reality was gut-wrenching.

It all came flooding back to him: his stupidity in not being more careful on the trail to Fort Hardin, his futile attempts to escape the Indians, his ultimate capture. His jaw tightened. The dirty trick they had played on him angered and embittered him. His lack of discernment had cost him dearly. And the warriors weren't finished with him yet. This was only the beginning. He didn't even want to speculate about what would happen the next day. All he knew was that they had been making plans last night—big plans.

He lifted his chin and tried to still the throbbing in his head and body. The clanging that he had heard was the horses as they shook their ropes and clumped their hooves to keep warm in the cold night air. Some distance away he saw a raccoon walking past. Jace envied it its freedom.

Sleep had left him abruptly, and now he could only stare into the frozen night. It was a painful and lonely vigil as he sat there until morning. No doubt it was the last night he would spend on this earth. Jace tried to think of Prudence, of the life they might have had together, but it was hard to keep his thoughts on her. Reality kept breaking in like an eager messenger. Wearily he tried to loosen his ropes, but they were too tight and too thick, and he was too weak. The gash at the back of his head had opened from his movements, and the blood started to slide slowly down his neck. Jace didn't even care. Nothing much mattered anymore.

When dawn finally deigned to crawl out, it was dismal. The sun fought to make an appearance, but it showed only bleakly in the sky, cheating the earth of its expected warmth. The gray refused to leave the sky and hung gloomily over everything.

Now Jace could no longer keep away the uneasy thoughts. They hadn't killed him yet. That gave him a little hope—not much, but some. Moreover, he had seen the braves arguing about him around the fire last night. They seemed to be preparing for an early start. From this, Jace deduced they might have him run the gauntlet. That would mean several days' grace while the war party traveled to one of their villages. The women and children enjoyed joining in, clubbing the enemy.

Nevertheless, it would also mean time for his wounds to heal. More important, he might find a means to escape along the way. Jace's spirits began to lift a little around the edges, despite the unencouraging start to the day.

When the sun was fully up, the Shawnee slowly climbed out of their blankets and coaxed the fire back to life. Some of its warmth reached out to Jace, and his blood began to flow once more. A sliver of optimism took root, even if it was not destined to last long.

The Indians were in a foul mood. They talked together and glared accusingly at Jace. They seemed to blame him for the lack of sun and the general dampness of the air. Their leader in particular was in bad humor. He kept rubbing his wounded shoulder, which had not improved from sleeping on the rubbled ground. He snarled at the others back and forth until they came to a decision. For the first time his grunts held a little satisfaction. He pulled his knife from its sheath. He looked across at Jace. Then he came striding over.

The sliver of hope broke into pieces. Jace could only stare dumbly as the brave approached. When he reached Jace, he stood there, feet spread apart, holding his knife. He looked at Jace. Jace stared back steadily. Black eyes clashed with hazel. The knife flickered a little. Jace tensed, waiting for it to cut into him. For timeless seconds the blade remained poised in front of his stiff face, doing its work on Jace's nerves. The air cracked with tension. Around them, the other Indians were silent, watching.

Suddenly the knife flashed. Jace could feel the cold steel touch his wrists. He drew in his breath. It slashed through the ropes that held him; then it sliced through the ones binding his feet. At once, miraculously, he was free.

But not for long.

The others lunged forward and roughly hauled him to his feet. His legs were wobbly and unable to hold him up. He slumped to the ground. Jace sat, taking valuable time to massage the life back into his legs while the Indians hovered like vultures over a carcass, afraid that if he moved even inches away, he might be out of their reach.

The leader, impatient with the time they were wasting, rapped out an order. Jace was dragged to his feet once more. A few men hurried away to where the horses were kept. There was an immediate stirring of hooves and wild thrashing in that direction. Then a horse was led into camp. It was the white stallion again. Jace remembered it from yesterday; it had trampled the Indian Jace had shot on the trail with a well-placed lead ball.

Jace frowned with puzzlement as they brought the horse over. It was plain that the animal wasn't Indian-bred. He fought the ropes all the way into camp, stomping on the ground and snorting. He was frightened. He didn't like the fire. Backing away from the Indians, he shook his mane.

Four men held him until they finally steadied the horse. The leader's black eyes went to Jace. He smiled. Jace looked at the men holding the fractious horse, the other Indians watching him interestedly, and suddenly enlightenment blinded him: they were going to tie him to the horse. The blood pounded in his head. He had heard of men being tied onto horses with a loop around their neck. When the horse ran, the man either held on or was strangled. Occasionally the rider lost his grip on the horse and fell to the ground, to be dragged until his neck broke.

There was to be no gauntlet. No more precious days of life left. No more chance for escape once he was placed on that horse. There was only one way he was getting off—dead. Jace slewed around and punched the Indian closest to him in the gut. Another one opened his mouth to yell, and Jace drilled his fist into the warrior's face. Two others jumped back, dismayed. None had expected their tractable prisoner to display so much energy. Jace elbowed them aside and headed for the forest. The leader shouted a warning, and they fell on him.

Jace didn't care. He waded in slugging. He fought like a wildcat with a strength he didn't know he possessed. One tall bird danced past Jace's fists and landed a hit on the back of his head. The scalp wound widened, and blood ran down his face. Jace bunched up his fist and slammed it into the man's side. The warrior gasped and fell, but three more took his place. One grabbed his arm and twisted it enthusiastically up, as if it was a pump handle. His friend, with pebbles for eyes, tossed a loop of rawhide around the wrist.

Jace commenced to kick at them, but the ornery Pebble-Eyes held on to that wrist like a dog holding on to a meaty bone. Another enterprising warrior, believing Jace to be occupied, tried to take his other wrist. Jace's hand smashed up. Bones broke. The man howled and fell away, holding his nose. In the end it was no use. Jace put up a good fight, but he was outnumbered.

His flailing fists were subdued, and the horse was brought back. All at once he was lifted high into the air and hoisted, backward, onto the wild stallion. They secured his legs under the animal's belly. Then they dropped a thick loop around his neck and pulled it tight. The other end of the rope was bound around the horse's neck. The leader made a grunt of approval deep in his throat.

The jittery stallion bucked a little as the rope was secured around its neck. "Easy boy," Jace called quaveringly. Already the cord was tightening painfully around Jace's throat. "Easy."

The Indians stepped back quickly, away from the frisky hooves. The stallion leaped forward, not liking Jace on his back nor the cord. He reared, then kicked sideways at the Indians, trying to flip Jace off. Jace grabbed at the mane with his hands, tilting his head back to stop the sudden constriction of his windpipe. The chief lifted his voice in a shrill command, and the Indians slapped the horse on its flanks. Immediately the stallion reared, then took off running. The Indians hurried to their horses to follow, none wishing to miss a single moment of enjoyment.

The trees whipped past Jace. One slashed him across the cheek. Jace ducked his head as a branch nearly gouged out his eyes. It cut a groove across his temple instead. The world went black for a second as the cord cut off his air, then air came rushing back into his lungs as the stallion leaped over some brush.

The stallion's breathing was loud, pulsing through Jace like the beating of a war drum. Everything was a blur of motion accompanied by tremendous pain. Jace's body pitched and jerked; his head flopped back and forth. He alternately blacked out and came to in seconds. During the long ride he thought his skull would explode.

But he was tougher than he thought. Time passed— time during which the horse raced through grasslands and forests. The sky reeled above him, and the trees spun out of control. All Jace heard was the thunder of hooves and the screaming of the Indians. Time meant nothing. Jace didn't even notice the sun traveling across the sky. All he could think of was to keep hold of that wiry mane, make sure his head was held stiffly, and grip hard on the horse's stomach.

Then they were flying across open prairie. Cutter's eyes bulged out; dust filled his mouth. The lathered horse was becoming more difficult to grip with his legs. His strength was almost depleted. He knew he couldn't hold on much longer. He looked to the heavens in silent prayer for what he thought would be the last time.

The horse carried him under a tree. It was a lone tree on a desolate plain. Above him, through a leafy patch, Jace saw what he thought to be a pair of bright blue eyes. He looked again, and they were gone. The stallion kept carrying him farther and farther away.

Chapter Eleven

Stiff-faced, Captain Tom Maxcy and his rangers sat around their cold camp in grim dejection. Several wearying days had been spent following the trail of the Shawnee war party. Several times they had thought they would catch up with them, but the Indians always managed to lose them. They were taking Dave Merrill someplace, and they didn't want anyone to find out where. Right now the rangers had lost the scent and didn't know where to begin again.

"If we don't find Dave soon," one of the men said, "it's gonna be too late. Three days since we lost them. Three days! I wouldn't like to predict his chances of comin' out of this alive."

Sam Logan let out his breath in worry. "No sign of

157

them Shawnee that I can see. It's like they disappeared into thin air."

"But they were takin' him someplace," Maxcy pointed out. "Otherwise they would have killed him right off. They were taking him someplace, and it wasn't back to their home. It's around here—I can feel it. I just don't know where."

"Timber Wolf Pass?" Jean Laurier, the Frenchman, asked.

"I don't know where that is," Maxcy returned. "No one does."

"It's just a myth," Sam Logan remarked.

"The Indians speak of it always," Jean interjected. "It exists. It is still used. Many are rumored to have been killed up there. No white man ever comes back."

A growing uneasiness washed over everyone. They didn't like to speak of Timber Wolf Pass. All had heard of what happened up there.

"A great warrior like Dave Merrill—him, they would want to kill in a style that is grand. Timber Wolf Pass would be a fitting place to take him," Jean went on.

"Mebbe they don't know who they're dealin' with," Nash Winslow said slowly.

"Everyone knows Dave Merrill. The very wind blows his name," Jean stated.

They all agreed sadly. "He's still got a chance. Mebbe his poor old soul ain't flown to heaven yet," Nash suggested. "Be a real shame if it has."

"Ford's just wouldn't seem the same without Dave.

He wasn't a drinkin' man, but he was a fightin' man and a talkin' man, and danged good at both," Sam Logan declared.

Everyone commenced to talk about Dave in the past tense, as if all present assumed they were on a lost mission.

"Now, I wonder," Nash Winslow ruminated aloud, "if he woulda married the widda."

"I bet he would have," Duke Jordan said, daringly. "I heard he went visiting her a few times and came back with doughnuts, pies, and suchlike."

"I do not know." Jean Laurier shook his head. "He was a proud dog and a wild one. He liked to have the whole country to wander in. I do not believe he would tie himself down to one place."

"He give me his bread and molasses t'other day." Monty spoke up in the gloom. "He always was a generous man, and that's all I'm prepared to say about him." He wiped his eyes with a dirty sleeve.

"He sure did love his bread and molasses," Maxcy agreed.

"Sure do hope they have some where he's a-goin'," Monty added fervently.

"Let's see if we can find his remains. Be a fine thing to at least bring 'em back to the widda. Give her somethin' to put a tombstone over," Nash Winslow said.

"Do you know if he had any family?" Maxcy asked the other men. They all looked at one another; everyone shook his head.

Duke spoke up. "He mentioned an Aunt Mirtha once. Spiritual sort of woman, always whuppin' the hell outta him when he was a boy."

"No wonder he turned out to be such a good man," Winslow commented.

"Is she still alive?"

"Wouldn't reckon so. He said somethin' about the angels reclaiming their own," Duke said reverently.

There was a somber silence. Suddenly Sam Logan shouted, "It's a damn shame—go out to get a man and only come back with his remains. It's a damn shame, that's what I say!"

"We all say it." Jean Laurier jumped to his feet and raised his cup of coffee. "Let us all drink a toast to Dave Merrill, the proud dog! May the red devils never catch up to him in the Great Beyond!"

They all rose to their feet. "To the proud dog!"

Maxcy added in a deep voice resonating with pain and sadness, "To He-Who-Cannot-Be-Caught!" They all wiped a tear away before lapsing into silence. For the rest of the evening they contemplated their dearly departed friend. They hoped he had had a quick and painless death . . . but they rather doubted it.

Dave's smooth, long strides carried him quickly across the landscape, vaulting him easily over fallen trees and streams. Knowing he had lost the war party, he felt he could maintain this pace for hours. By tomorrow night he might be seeing Angie.

Toward late afternoon Dave was driven by hunger to find sustenance. He came upon a mass of blueberry bushes, so he sat down and ate his fill. There were also some black walnut trees, and Dave spent some time cracking open the nuts that were scattered all around.

When he'd had enough, he was on his way, thinking he had a clear run to the fort. It was something of a shock when he felt, through the soles of his feet, the drumming of fast-moving ponies. He knew very well that the party chasing him was elsewhere, beating the bushes and wearing out their moccasins trying to find him. It must be another party of them varmints, and these on horseback.

Dave knew he had to make himself scarce. Where he was now, on a practically bald heath with nary a tree in sight, he'd be a pretty target for them critters. Then Dave spotted it: a rotten elm several hundred years old. It stood, tall but solitary, and was the only cover available. Dave made straight for it. He wasn't particular.

As he scrambled up, he spied a big hole in the upper trunk. Why, that hole was just made in heaven for Dave! He'd skedaddle down in and be snug as a flea. Eagerly Dave shinnied up the tree and looked down the hole. It was big and cavernous and would fit him neatly. Good thing he hadn't eaten that many doughnuts. Dave straddled the opening and prepared to lower himself down. Through the musty darkness a stark, white face stared up at him. Dave's eyes goggled at the sightless holes in the face. Its wide mouth was dropped agape, all ready to howl out in fear. It was then that Dave realized it was a skull. Someone else had gotten there ahead of him a long time ago.

"Boilin' oats," he muttered. "The dang thing's already occupied." There was no room for a second person.

Horses were already trampling through the woodsy fringe and crashing down among a swarm of bushes and brambles that clogged the way to the heath. Dave knew he had to act quickly. Since the hole was already full up, he grasped the limb above him and heaved himself up. Then Dave lay on his stomach along its thick, tilted length, flattening his lean body to its contours. He hoped he was high enough to be out of line of vision, because the danged tree was old, broken down, and nearly bare of leaves. Fact was, the big branch he was on was mighty shaky and shot through with fractures. Dave's weight on it made it groan with pain. Dave sympathized with it and encouraged it to stay in one piece—at least till the Indians passed.

Fortunately, the Indians were not looking for Dave, or they surely would have found him. They were engaged in other sport: another white man. Dave huddled closer, and the limb sqeaked ominously.

They had tied this other man onto a horse, a beautiful white one, that flew across the ground prodded along by screaming warriors. To the back and facing the tail, a man was tied on by his neck and ankles. Every time the horse jumped or sped up, that noose pulled tighter around his throat. There was nothing he could do about it but try to hold on.

"Mercy me, that poor soul!" Dave felt sorry for him. He'd heard about this torture but never from anyone who'd lived through it. Unless someone intervened, it was certain death. Dave hoped it was no one he knew.

The Indians shouted louder as they raced toward the tree. Dave hunkered down. The half-rotted limb creaked agitatedly and swayed from the movement.

The rider was jostled from side to side but, miraculously, managed to stay on. "Good for you," Dave muttered. He couldn't quite see the face yet. All that was visible was a head of dark hair. The party came on. Dave held his breath. All were watching the white horse; no one noticed the old elm. Then they were directly under him. The vibrations from the pounding hooves and the echoing of the screams set the branch to quivering. Dave stopped breathing as a distinct cracking struck his ears. Still he kept his eyes on the white man. He must see who he was.

The group roared under him, storming for the woods ahead. Dave looked down on the stallion. The white man threw his head back for a second and looked up. Dave recognized the deathly pale countenance of Jace Cutter! Hazel eyes met blue for one startling second, then Jace was gone as the horse kicked up its heels and ran in fear. The whole bunch trampled wildly for the trees. Then they disappeared, leaving clouds of dust that flew up into Dave's face. He gagged, and the whole branch suddenly had enough of him and fell. The last Indian had vanished into the forest when the branch clattered to the ground and tossed Dave off. He rolled and scrambled for cover. The heath was empty. The Indians had not seen Dave nor heard the branch break. He sneaked out again, relieved.

He was safe, but Jace was not. How Jace had fallen into the Shawnee's hands was more than Dave could fathom. Of course it was his sworn duty as a ranger to try to save him. Dave wouldn't have even entertained a notion not to. Jace was his friend too, even if he was a sneakin' to the widow behind his back. He had to try to help him. First, though, he'd have a look at that tree trunk. Might be something there he could use to save Jace. Right now, he was plumb out of ideas.

Dave climbed back up that tree again almost as fast as he had tumbled out of it.

He commenced to look into the tree's cavity to see what his clumsiness had uncovered. A veritable treasure trove of bones and oddities lay before his astonished eyes. Where to begin? The first thing he picked up was the skull, white and bleached with time.

"At last, a friendly face," Dave said with satisfaction.

Dave just plain liked to talk, so he commenced to talk to that skull. He was a natural-born listener, that skull was, so they hit it off at once. Dave chided it for being in the trunk in the first place.

"Ain't ya got no sense? How'd ya get yourself stuck in here, anyway?" he asked as he leaned down, digging in the rotted insides of the tree. "Oh, I see. Got your foot caught, huh? Couldn't get it undone. No room. I believe that. It's possible. I seen it happen before, but I got to tell ya the truth: it never happened to me. Though there are stories I could tell ya—" He broke off as he found other items: a tomahawk—rusty but useable; a knife; some beads—blue ones. They would look nice around Angie's neck. He put them aside. Deeper down he found a small leather sack with fixings for making a fire. He put the rest of his treasures into the sack.

As an afterthought he added the two skeletal hands. "I might have a use for them," he confided to the skull. "Ya never can tell. And even if I don't, well, it's comfortin' to know ya got your hands as well. When ya got your head and your hands, why, ya don't need much of anything else."

Dave tied up the bag and lowered himself out of the tree, clutching his loot. The necklace, Dave intended as a gift for Angie. With her curly brown hair and slender neck, the beads would look mighty fine a-layin' on her bosom. Dave blushed at such ungentlemanly thoughts, but he couldn't help entertaining them anyway. Up on Timber Wolf Pass, he hadn't dared think of her or their future, but now he was free to lavish his thoughts upon her. His thoughts, however, were not all pleasant. There was still the matter of that doughnut-eatin' Jace. Sure, he was one of Dave's best friends, and he loved him like a brother. But there was no denying that he possessed all the accoutrements of a widow-stealer.

He surely hoped Angie wasn't partial to him. Jace had been drapin' himself about her place all them weeks. Dave frowned for a moment with real worry, then brightened. Angie had kissed *him,* hadn't she? Come to think on it, he had done all of the kissing, but she didn't seem to mind—not at all!

"And Angie cried when I left." Dave spoke aloud as he tucked the skull under his arm. "Imagine a woman cryin' over me!" He seemed satisfied. "Ain't no one cried over me since my Aunt Mirtha, and I think them were tears of rage, God rest her soul. Angie's my girl," Dave explained companionably. "Don't know why I'm tellin' ya so much." Somehow that danged skull had a way of charming the words right out of his mouth.

He had to save Jace, of course. That was understood. Dave wouldn't think of doing anything else. He studied the trail that led across the clearing and back to the trees.

"We'll just walk in their wake; then no one will know we're a-followin' them. Might be more of their kind around. Fact is, I know there is. What do ya think?" The skull seemed to agree with Dave. "We'd best hustle our hocks. I'm thinkin' they'll be making camp soon. Them horses of theirs were mighty played out. When we get there, well, we'll discuss what we got to do."

Having reached this agreement amicably, he broke

into a long-legged stride, busy with his own thoughts while he tracked Jace. The sun began to drop toward the ground, taking its light with it, but he pushed on. Soon Dave heard small noises and talking.

"They're campin' for the night," he informed his new friend, who might not have noticed this fact. "Now, I've been doin' me some considerin' as we was walkin' along, and I come up with a plan." He looked down at the inquisitive face under his arm.

"I got a job for ya to do, and I'd better tell ya right off—ya won't like it. It's no use your frownin' at me, though. It's got to be done."

At a safe distance from the Indian camp, he set the skull down and began to collect firewood. He constructed a big circle of kindling and placed the skull down tenderly in the middle of it.

"Now you just set yourself right there and don't move. You're catchin' on, ain't ya?" He then proceeded to place the skeletal hands in front of it, crossing them in an attitude of restfulness. He artistically entwined them with one of the strings of bear claws taken from his lately lamented adversary. "He'd be proud for you to have 'em," Dave assured him. Finally he stuck two long, stout pieces of wood into the eye sockets.

"Right pretty," he admired. "When they see ya just a-glowin' and a-cracklin'," he assured him, "why, the fear of hellfire will enter their worthless souls. They'll be plumb scared of you. They'll think you're Bear Claw a-comin' back from the dead!" He chuckled at his own ingenuity. "Don't know how I come to think these things, but it's right clever. And it's no use your givin' me them blamed looks. I should think you'd want to be fearsome in their eyes. What're they gonna think of a man stupid enough to get hisself caught in a tree and then die of it? You ought to be thankin' me just about now."

When he was finished to his satisfaction, he got out his newly acquired tinder box with flint, steel, and tinder, and soon he had a cheerful fire started. He lighted the piles of wood around the skull, then torched the two pieces of kindling sticking out of the eye sockets.

"Ain't you a sight? There now. Danged if ya don't scare me some. Now you just wait there and don't move." He paused a moment. "Well, I'm gonna miss ya. Don't recollect when I taken to someone so fast. We had some good conversations, you and me, but your friends will take good care of ya. They got to. They'll be too afraid not to. See ya some fine day!" Dave saluted him respectfully and turned away.

Dave left and crept through the woods to where the Indians were making camp. He saw Jace right away, tied to a tree. A bowl of water he couldn't possibly reach was a few feet away from him.

"Tormentin' devils," he muttered.

Suddenly the smell of smoke drifted in from the fire Dave had made. At first the Indians didn't notice. Then one young buck began to bark loudly. He pointed in the direction from which Dave had come. A thin snake of smoke had begun to wind up into the air, visible against the clear night sky. They all turned, grunting and talking. It could be an enemy, but it could be a friend. Some of them slipped into the woods. Others followed. Soon there was only one warrior left to guard Jace.

Dave enjoyed imagining those bucks sneaking up on that big old fire, 'hawks ready, preparing to pounce on an enemy. Then they'd see that old skull a-grinnin' and burnin', and they'd commence to shake and shiver with fright, particularly when they saw Bear Claw's necklace. Bear Claw was a well-known fella, to hear him braggin', so Dave was pretty sure they'd see that there necklace and know the skull for him. How they'd cry and moan! How they'd beg them old ancestors not to do the same thing to them! Only they'd be grovelin' at the feet of the wrong person. It should be Dave Merrill's feet at the bottom of it all. Dave Merrill, Indian-whipper, who should be gettin the credit. *Ah, me,* Dave sighed, *life is durned unfair.*

Pushing these contemplations aside, Dave went on over to rescue Jace. He'd best get going before them Indians started to think. On silent feet he crept up behind the guard who was mending a moccasin. Dave used the dull end of his 'hawk to whack the man on the head. The man fell into a senseless heap.

Jace looked up at the noise and seemed amazed at the sight of the collapsed Indian. Dave moved so silently and swiftly through the shadows that Jace never saw him make the strike or circle around the camp to stand behind him. Yet almost at once he felt the bonds holding him fall away from his arms and legs. He turned and saw the dancing blue eyes of Dave Merrill.

"Dave!" A crooked smile twisted Jace's face. "I thought it was you for a second there, but I didn't know if I was imagining things or not. I thought I was going crazy from lack of food and water." He leaned down and took up the bowl of water at his feet and drank from it thirstily.

"Well, maybe ya are," Dave acknowledged, "but here I am, and I think we ought to get outta here fast afore them Injuns get tired of lookin' at that old skull. Not that he ain't quaint-lookin'."

Jace's face was blank as he moved his feet to get the blood flowing. "How did you get them away? Did you say *skull*?" He groaned from the sudden rush of blood through his cramped muscles.

"I'll tell ya later," Dave promised. And Jace knew he meant it.

With a hasty retreat uppermost in his mind, Dave flew into action. He gathered food and weapons from the camp, careful to take a little from everyone so no one would notice right away. Jace, already mounted on an Indian pony, was untying the white stallion to lead it out of there.

"Not that horse, Jace," Dave said. "That horse can be seen too easy, and anyway, he's all played out."

"I'm taking him with me," Jace muttered stubbornly. "If I don't, there's no telling what they'll do to him. I like this horse."

Dave understood. "I know what ya mean," he said, flinging himself onto the back of a roan. "Had me a yeller dog once. Best friend I ever had. Anyone ever try to lay a hand on that dog in anger, why I just upped and showed them their mistake. No one ever made it twice." He patted the roan's neck. "Let's ride."

They walked the horses for a short distance, then picked up the pace. They rode all night and only stopped as pink dawn painted the sky, and they could see forbidding storm clouds building up in the west.

"Coming this way soon," Dave predicted. "Best find a place to rest. Don't matter now. When that rain sets in, them Injuns won't find our tracks at all." Jace wearily agreed. Tucked away against a wall of jutting ledges, Dave located a cave big enough for their horses. Hurriedly they gathered wood and were just able to make it back with a few armloads before the rain came slapping down.

Dave got some jerky out of his pack and handed it to Jace, who was almost too tired to eat but took it anyway.

"Listen, Dave, I want to thank you for saving my life," Jace said embarrassedly, combing agitated fingers through his dirty hair.

"Don't mention it," Dave said modestly, knowing that back at the fort, his rescue of poor old Jace would figure among his best tales.

"I mean it. I've thought a lot of bad things about you"—he stopped, then added with reluctance—"and said them too."

"Well, I thought a lot of bad things about you too," Dave admitted. "Fact is, I'm still thinkin' 'em." He turned to Jace, his usually good-humored brow knitted into a frown. "I sure am thinkin' what a no-good, two-timin' widda-stealer ya are. 'Course, I know Angie—er, Mrs. Wright—is a mighty good-lookin' woman, and ya might be gettin' fantastical ideas about her marryin' ya, but I'm here to say that ya got to go through me first. That's how I feel. So I want to know what ya think about it." Dave seemed to be getting almost belligerent.

"Whoa!" Jace held up a hand, smiling. "I admit Mrs. Wright is pretty."

"She's more than that!"

"All right, beautiful. And she's a good woman."

"Amen to that." Dave nodded in agreement.

"But, you see, I've met someone else." He turned a bit pink under Dave's blue-eyed scrutiny.

"Someone else? Who? There ain't no one at the fort you're interested in. When did ya meet her?"

"Her name is Prudence," Jace said, smiling in that foolish way a man does when he's in love with an angel. "Prudence Dooley."

Frankly Dave couldn't see how anyone could favor another girl after seeing Angie, but he was willing to be credulous. "When did ya meet her?" Dave was astounded, and his belligerence melted.

"You know that little girl who threw rocks at everyone?"

"Her, I remember," Dave said with little enthusiasm.

"Well, she has a sister," Jace added.

"I hope *she* don't throw rocks."

"Of course not. Prudence Dooley is beautiful and sweet and gentle. And I'm going to marry her." His voice was filled with anger and desperation. He went on to tell Dave his story.

"Thank you for your confidences," Dave replied, flattered to be the recipient. "I heard plenty about Big Bull Tuttle. He's a land-stealer, him and his no-account brothers. He chases people off their land, then claims it for his own."

"Prudence said that Bull took Ned Potter's land, and Hadley's too," Jace reported. "Potter had come out three years ago with a wife and four children. Bull trampled his newly planted crops, set fire to his barn, and stole their livestock. The Potters left to build someplace else. Bull claimed the land and said Potter had sold it to him. Miss Prudence has a nice homestead, and Bull wants her and the land. I've got to get back there to see what's happened. I left Riley Wiggins there, but he's no match for the likes of those three."

"Riley's as smart as paint," Dave pointed out. "Well, I remember—"

"We should get moving. See how Prudence is," Jace said, frustrated, kicking at the fire and not wishing to hear one of Dave's stories just now.

"When this rain lets up, we'll go," Dave promised. "But while we're about it, we'll be passin' through some of Bull's newly acquired property, won't we?"

"I suppose." Jace shrugged.

"I got me to thinkin' that if Bull Tuttle can put his name on the land and just take it, why, so can we. Won't no one be the wiser," Dave predicted sagely.

Chapter Twelve

The next morning Jace Cutter and Dave Merrill came around a sharp bend in the trail that hugged the contours of an abrupt rise. "Come on, Jace," Dave prodded. "Time's a-wastin'." He pulled up and scanned the trees before him. "Are we on Hadley land yet?"

"Yes, this is Hadley Hill, part of the homestead. Beyond it is Miss Prudence's holdings."

"Give a look there." Dave pointed to an ash towering a good seventy feet into the sky, high above the others. "See that white gash on its trunk about six feet up?" Jace nodded, noticing the bark chipped away. "There was somethin' carved there to tell whose land it is, but it's been hacked up. It was probably Hadley's mark. Now look up another five feet by that big branch. Ya see that cut? It's fresher than the first. Hadley cleared out about a month ago. That higher mark is somebody else's. It's fresh, only about a week old."

"Looks like someone is already claiming this land."

Dave had seen tomahawk marks before, but this was different. Someone had used his 'hawk to obliterate the Hadley mark, then carve his own mark higher up. Dave had seen that before too; it was called landstealing.

"I'll go see whose mark it is." 'Hawk and knife in his belt, Dave shinnied up until he reached the new gash. He looked down, grinning. "It's a T all right!"

"Bull Tuttle. That's his sign." Jace frowned. "Miss Prudence said the Tuttles were using heavy-handed tactics to scare people off their claims. I guess she was right about Hadley."

"Always had a hankerin' for my own land. Be a right nice weddin' present for—well, a certain person." Dave blushed, then got back to the work at hand. "Think I'll claim it for myself." Dave proceeded to chip away at the letter *T* until it was gone. He climbed up a few more feet and began carving away. "I'll put an *M* here for *Merrill*. Let that old woolly varmint try to climb up here and get rid of it!" He chuckled.

When finished, Dave jumped down. "Let's claim the whole piece of land."

Jace glanced about apprehensively as Dave worked his way up two more trees at each corner of the property. He had an uneasy feeling but couldn't say why. When Dave started up the last tree, Jace tried to stop him.

"We don't have time, Dave. We've got to get to Prudence's house."

"I'll always have time to annoy Bull Tuttle," he chortled. "Now, you just stay put there and keep watch whilst I finish up. Ya know, Jace, there's a lot of good ash trees here," he called down as he eradicated Bull's final sign of ownership. "I like to make my bows and arrows from ash. But of course Osage orange is best for bows. Why, I seen it used amongst the Mohawk and even as far west as Cahokia."

Jace looked about again. He thought he'd detected a movement, but nothing stirred in the woods.

"I once stuck my bow into the ground for safekeeping and came back a few weeks later. Danged if it didn't start to take root and send out shoots," Dave went on in a droning voice.

Jace found it hard to pay attention—so much so that he missed the whispering sound of someone creeping up behind him.

"Did I ever tell ya about the time I was treed by four Miami?"

Jace couldn't reply. A thick, hairy arm came around his throat, cutting off his warning cry to Dave. Another hand stuffed a cloth into his mouth, while still another began to bind his wrists. Shaking the hair from his eyes,

Jace managed to twist around and look at his captors. His eyes widened. It was Big Bull Tuttle. Two other men were with him—a weedy youth with a mean look, and an oafish man in his midtwenties with a broad chest and small head. The family resemblance among them was painfully apparent.

"Well, that's done," Dave declared loudly. "I'd sure like to see Big Bull Tuttle's ugly face when he finds out that I'm a-claimin' his land. That sure will be a sight." Dave chuckled as he climbed down, not at all warned by the silence of his companion.

Dave jumped the last few feet and turned around. He found himself looking into Bull Tuttle's furious red face.

"Well, Merrill." Tuttle grabbed him by the front of his jacket and yanked him closer. "You wanted to see my face—now take a good look at it," he snarled.

"Why, Bull, I was mistook. You ain't near as ugly as ya used to be." Dave smiled at him placatingly.

Bull drew his fist back and stung Dave's face with his knuckles.

Blood spurted from Dave's mouth. He grinned at Tuttle, wiping away the blood with his palm. "Don't hold all that bad temper in, Bull—it's unhealthy."

Tuttle punched him again.

"Tie 'em up, and don't be too easy on 'em!" he yelled to the oaf, who obeyed. Bull turned his attention to Jace.

"So you're still alive, are ya? Thought when I seed

them Injuns takin' out after ya that you was a goner."
His suspicious eyes slid to Dave. Dave smiled back benignly. To Jace he said, "Shoulda shot ya when I had the
chance. Oh, yeah, you were in my sights when them Injuns appeared. Thought they was savin' me some trouble, but I guess I gotta do things myself."

"Hey, Bull." Clip was squinting up at the tree Dave
had just been fiddling with. "Lookee up there. That's
what they was doin'! Your mark is gone. It's plumb
gone!" Bull barreled over to the tree and climbed up a
few feet. He dropped down, his big face furious.

"So you're tryin' to steal my land away," he growled.

"*Your* land?" Dave queried. "You got proof you
own it?"

"You want proof? Here's my proof!" He doubled
his fist and drove it into Dave's lean stomach. "Do *you*
want to see my proof too, Cutter?"

Jace declined the invitation, but Bull showed him
anyway. A grunt flew out of Jace's mouth as Bull landed
a blow to his jaw.

Bull stood back and watched them with malicious
enjoyment. "Want any more proof? I thought not. Hey,
boys," he invited the others to listen. "See who we got
here by the tail? He-Who-Cannot-Be-Caught. Leastways, that's what some call him. Looks like you're
captured sure enough, slack-jaw!" Bull crowed. "Some
ranger you are! Us bein' nobodies—so you think—and
us capturin' the likes of you as easy as scrapin' cow
dung offen our feet."

"Reckon ya got plenty to scrape off," Dave said critically.

"Shut up! All them stories you're always tellin' about yourself must be a lot of hot air. He-Who-Cannot-Be-Caught!" he guffawed. "Them Shawnee musta been lookin' the other way!"

"Iffen I was to tell ya how I was occupyin' myself the last few days, you would be amazed," Dave said. "How I wrastled the illustrious Bear Claw—and him with a load of them around that thick neck of his—how I wrastled him offen the mountain and left his body smashed down below on the rocks. Iffen I was to tell ya all of it, you'd wake up screamin' with the night shakes."

"We're wastin' time listenin' to his bellyful of lies! I ain't one of them old codgers ya gull over to Ford's while they're a-settin' around swillin' Monongahela water by the jugful. I'm a sight smarter than they are."

"I knowed that. I could tell just by lookin' at ya. Now let me tell ya—"

"Don't tell me nothin'! I ain't got time nor the stomach to hear your ranting. Get these bums to camp afore I kick the livin' daylights outta them. Vole, get their horses. Come on, let's move. I got things to do today."

Clip led them back to the Tuttle camp.

It was quite a setup. There was plenty of food, ammunition, and supplies. It was also close to Prudence's land—closer even than Bull Tuttle's cabin was. Both

Merrill and Cutter figured the Tuttles were up to something big.

Jace and Dave were shoved down onto a log, still tied up. The Tuttles, hungry now, prepared to eat. A big pot was hanging over their fire.

Dave smelled the food, and his stomach curled into a rigid ball. Them blueberries were long gone. A piece of meat would suit him just fine. He hadn't had any in days.

The Tuttles did not invite them to partake of their fare. Each one scooped up a brimming ladleful of stew and crammed it down. Bull stood in front of the two men and chewed on a chunk of meat with gusto. Anything that happened to run down his chin, he wiped up with the back of his hand.

"You two haven't met my brothers proper-like yet, have ya? This here is Clip." Clip stopped eating long enough to give them a cold stare from under shaggy brows. "And this here's the youngest, Vole." Vole was about sixteen years old, tall and long-armed, with mean eyes and a vacant expression on his face.

Vole placed his plate on the ground and picked up his knife. He stared at Dave, seemingly fascinated by him. Vole rubbed his knife, a long, slender, deadly looking affair, but it was already shiny and spotless. This way and that he turned it, while the blade caught and flashed the light. He smiled at it as if in a trance. Then he looked up suddenly at Dave. No doubt about it. The lad had taken a rare fancy to him, Dave thought.

Vole jumped up and flung the knife at Dave's head.

Dave pulled back, and the blade sank deep into the tree trunk Dave had been leaning against. It quivered so hard, he could hear the humming in his ears. "Boilin' oats!" Dave yelped.

"Stop that, Vole! This ain't no time for funnin' around," Bull growled, finishing his meal.

"I don't like them blue eyes a-starin' at me," Vole breathed raggedly. He retrieved his knife. As he leaned over Dave, his face promised more trouble later.

"That young shaver sure is quick with his knife!" Dave exclaimed. "Best keep a careful eye on him, Bull, or the next hide that knife goes into might not just be mine."

Bull became angry at the warning, all the more so because it was true. Vole was beginning to test his authority. Even now, the colorless eyes were watching his brother in a weighing manner. Vole knew the conversation was about him and seemed almost pleased with the fear he could invoke in his nearest and dearest.

"Vole, put that knife away," Bull ordered, not liking the way his brother was staring at him. Vole continued to rub his fingers over the knife handle.

"Here," Clip intervened, "use it on this gourd." He tossed Vole a large gourd, which landed by his feet.

Immediately Vole began to stab and slash it with his blade. A grin curled the corners of his thin mouth.

Bull looked at him a long moment, then turned

away. A confrontation had been averted, but only barely. The day would come when a mere gourd would no longer satisfy Vole.

When Bull finished his meal, he sat down on a rock. Having eaten, he was now inclined to be expansive. "Yeah," he said to Jace, "when I seen them Injuns takin' after ya, I laughed but good. But don't think your still bein' alive will change anything. I'm takin' Prudence Dooley and her land. I don't know how ya managed to get away." He looked at Dave. "I can't believe *you* saved him." There was a lengthy silence. That in itself was strange. "Well, speak up! The Delaware call you the Talkin' Otter, so start talkin'!" He kicked Dave in the shin. It unloosed his tongue.

"Yeah, I saved him all right," Dave replied. "No tongue can tell what I been through since I was took by them Injuns and saved Jace in a miraculous manner. And if you'll just set there, I might be persuaded to tell ya my incredulible tale of—"

Another twanging noise ripped through the air, and Bull jumped to his feet. Vole was standing up, staring excitedly into the woods. His knife was stuck in a tree trunk.

"What the devil ya doin' now, Vole?" Bull rapped out.

"A cricket! I seen me a cricket! Don't like crickets. Hate that chirpin'."

"Ain't that a cricket crawlin' up Bull's leg?" Dave asked promptly.

Eyes agleam, Vole turned to survey his brother's pants leg.

Bull's eyes widened, and he beat Vole to the knife, tearing it out of the tree trunk. "Leave that knife alone!" he hollered, sweating a little at Vole's quivering anger as Bull took his knife. Bull glared in Dave's direction.

"Just tryin' to help." Dave's voice was bland. "Him bein' afraid of crickets and all."

"Keep them lips buttoned, Merrill, or I'll rip 'em offen your face. Don't try to cause no trouble."

"Seems like ya already got it." Both noticed Vole creeping up behind his brother and reaching for the knife's handle that protruded from Bull's belt.

"Vole!" Bull hit his hand away, and Vole's colorless eyes shot fire. "Finish your gourd." He turned back to the two prisoners. "We're goin' now. I told ya we got things to do, so let me tell ya what they are, so's you can sit here and brood. We're goin' over to the Dooley house. We'll take care of that boy ya left in charge. Then Miss Prudence will be glad to have a man around, especially with you dead."

"I'm not dead," Jace put in.

Vole giggled.

"Hear Vole a-laughin'? Ya know why? 'Cause when we get back, you two are both gonna be dead. I'm only keepin' ya alive in case I need a hostage." He leaned forward. "Mayhap Miss Dooley will agree to marry me iffen I don't kill ya." He grinned as Jace's face turned white with fury. "Clip, you stay here. Vole can go with me."

"I want to stay here," Vole protested. "I don't trust them blue eyes. I don't like 'em a-watchin' me and a-watchin' me. . . ."

"You're comin' with me. You can have a go at that Riley boy. Remember him?"

Vole did. "Don't like him. Didn't like that girl with the freckles. I don't like freckled kids." He stopped. "I want my knife."

"You'll get it back when we get to the Dooley farm," Bull said irritably.

Vole had a one-track mind. "Now."

"When we get to the farm, and that's that."

Vole gave in with ill grace, kicking the butchered gourd and sending it into the trees.

"You, Clip, watch these two—watch 'em good. And if they try to escape, you have my permission to kill 'em. Especially this one." He gave Dave a kick. "He ain't called the Talkin' Otter for nothin'. So don't ya let him talk ya into lettin' him loose."

"What kind of fool do you think I be?"

"I'm just warnin' ya. Once he starts talkin', ya never know where you'll end up. He's as mesmerizin' as a man with two heads. And you know how mesmerizin' that can be!"

"I sure do!" Clip shouted eagerly.

The brothers gathered up their rifles and powder

horns. Bull still wore a frown on his face. "I got a real bad feelin', leaving these two—real bad. You just mind my words, Clip. You watch that Merrill. I'll be back as soon as may be." With one last parting scowl at Dave, Bull and Vole left the clearing, mounted up, and headed toward Dooley land.

Dave leaned back and relaxed. "Ya hear that, Jace? Bull feels real bad about leavin' us here, his guests. Fella shows fine feelings."

"You shut up." Clip's voice was short. "The only thing he feels bad about is leavin' you two still alive, but that won't be for long."

"Did ya kill Hadley for his land?" Dave asked casually. "Or Potter?"

"I didn't kill no one for their land," Clip snarled.

"I didn't think ya did. Ya got a real honest face on ya. I sure do hope that old Bull won't do nothin' to hurt Miss Prudence. I guess ya don't know that Jace, here, is engaged to her."

"Ha!" Clip broke off some bread and stuffed it into his mouth.

"I guess ya don't know that if Bull tries to hurt her or steal her land away, why, Jace here is gonna do somethin' about it."

"I will," Jace promised.

"Youse two are mighty big talkers for somebody who's trussed up like a pair of turkeys and ain't goin' nowhere." Clip spat out crumbs in derision.

"Big talkin' is the only kind I do. I reckon 'cause I

only do big things, me bein' the man I am. But never mind about me. Did I ever tell ya, Jace, about the time I fought forty Injuns? More like sixty, actual-like, when I got done, but I don't usually count the ones just layin' around on the ground wounded."

Jace professed not to know the story, even though he had heard it many times before. Dave commenced to tell his tale, dwelling on his resourcefulness, bravery, and just plain ingenuity in beating them off. "Oh, yeah, I coulda run, I guess, but I didn't think it fair to them Injuns, them bein' so set on fightin'." He looked at Clip, who stared back in stony silence.

"Bet ya never fought forty Injuns, did ya, Clip? Not many has, I confess, but that ain't nothin' to what happened to me a few days ago. Somethin' so horrible, so fearsome, so incredible, that I can scarce think on it without a-tremblin' in stupefaction. Ya see, I was taken up to Timber Wolf Pass and lived to tell of it. Yes, sir, you're a-lookin' at the first white man to survive it." Dave straightened his shoulders, expecting accolades.

"You're a liar," Clip shot out angrily.

"Untie me! Untie me now, and I'll show ya not to call Dave Merrill a liar!" Dave shouted, struggling at his bonds.

"I ain't untyin' ya," Clip said, putting on some coffee, "and ya are a liar. No one comes back from Timber Wolf Pass—not even you. So go stick your head in a pile of manure."

"Mighty fine thing to tell a livin' legend," Dave remarked, offended. "And since you're actin' so disagreeable, I won't tell ya about it."

"Good for you," Jace applauded.

"I'll just tell Jace here."

"You already told me," Jace said hastily.

"Some things is just worth hearin' again." Dave began. "Now you and I both know that no one never come down from Timber Wolf Pass alive until a certain ranger named Dave Merrill was took up there. Them Injuns raced after me in the woods, and I let 'em catch me. Yep, you heard me a-right! I let 'em! I won't tell ya why, 'cause that's the kind of modest and humble person I am. It involves a certain young lady. We'll get back to that later. But I got to tell ya, I sure led them Injuns on a ramble through the woods. And when I run up against some rocks, I knew I had to turn and fight. And fight I did. My powerful fists flung them Injuns left and right. There was plenty of blood a-flowin', and not all of it mine! Well, it took twenty of them red devils to finally wrastle me to the ground and tie me up. One big one—musta been all of six-feet-five—was a fella named Bear Claw. I told ya about him, but did I tell ya he had a necklace full of them claws around his red neck? Well, maybe he fought an old bear easy, but he needed all the rest of them friends of his to catch Dave Merrill. That Injun was mad as two nests of hornets and was proceedin' to cut my throat, when the rest of them realized my magnificence. They knowed me for He-

Who-Cannot-Be-Caught. So they took me up to Timber Wolf Pass to give me to them old ancestors of theirs. I'm talkin' about those ghostly warriors that haunt the place.

"They staked me out on the sacrificial stone—stark, ravin' nekked from the waist up—and left me there for a meal for the old folks. You can take the word of a man who's looked on 'em: them ghosts are real. Maybe someday I'll tell ya exactly how I outwitted them—if ya can take it." Dave let out his breath exhaustedly. "But I don't think ya can. If I was to tell ya all I encountered, you'd be a-tremblin' in dismay. Even now when I think on it, I have to admire my feats of courage. I not only got away from twenty fearsome Injuns, but I got away from their ancestors too. And that's somethin' no one's ever done." Dave leaned back, replete with satisfaction.

Clip said nothing. His lips were pressed tightly together. He was breathing heavily. Dave calculated that one more story would just about mentally disarrange Clip. Dave continued breezily. "I kind of remind myself of what Juliet Caesar once said. You remember Juliet Caesar, don't ya, Jace? Ya gave me this Shakespeare book once."

"I think you mean Julius Caesar," Jace said cautiously.

"That's right, now that I think on it, there were twins, weren't they, in that *Twelfth Night*—Juliet and Julius?" Dave beamed.

"There could have been." Jace didn't like to ruin Dave's story. He saw that, despite his pretending otherwise, Clip, though drinking coffee, was actually listening. Jace could tell because Clip's countenance became darker and darker. Jace hoped he wasn't prone to fits.

"Somethin' about bein' born great or achieving greatness. Then there's the ones that have it dang near thrust upon them. That's why I recollect it, 'cause that's me. I not only had greatness thrust upon me, but it ran down the road beatin' me over the head until I admitted I was great. I ain't afeared of bein' great no more—now I got myself used to it. And speakin' of great personages"— his face took on a warm glow of fond remembrance— "that reminds me of the time I was a month-old baby, still in my swaddlin' clothes, when a passel of Injuns attacked our farm. I can see by your face, Clip, that you're a-wonderin' what a mere suckling such as me could do. Well, I'll tell ya. Why, I just jumped outta my cradle, kicked it aside—I got real powerful legs, ya know—and grabbed up two rifles, one in each of my little paws. My face full of wildness, I tottered to the door, slamming it open with my bare head. With arrows a-flyin' this way and that, and my kinfolk a-hidin' behind my back, I stepped outside. My pa, locking the door behind me, tells me, 'Get to it, boy!' And I did. Them rifles were bigger than I was, I reckon, but when them Injuns seen me a-standin' there in all my fierceness and meanin' business, why, they got so scared, they commenced to run away and—"

"Shut up! Shut up!" Clip jumped up and threw his coffee to the ground.

Dave looked at Clip in surprise.

"I cain't stand that flannel mouth of yours a-goin' nonstop!" Clip was almost crying. "I'd like to beat your face in! I'd like to pull your hair out from here all the way to the fort!" His chest was heaving agitatedly as he choked out his threats.

Jace looked sideways at Dave, thinking he had gone too far, but Dave did not seem a bit scared. A perplexed expression sat on his face, as if he couldn't understand what the fuss was about. Dave turned his head slightly just then to look at Jace, and one eyelid came down in a wink.

"Well, now, what appears to be eatin' away at your innards, Clip?" Dave asked concernedly. "Were ya wonderin' if I lived through it all? Well, let me put your mind at rest—I did. Say now—maybe you're jealous?" he asked, as if the thought had just occurred to him. "Yeah, that makes more sense. Many men are, and I can't blame 'em—"

"Ya know what it is?" Clip sputtered. "It's you! It's torture listenin' to you jaw about yourself! No mortal man could abide it for long!" He strode to Dave and stood in front of him. "I'd like ta . . . I'd like ta . . ." His hands clenched and unclenched.

"Like ta what?" Dave asked interestedly. "Give me a cup of coffee? Sounds mighty fine."

"I'd like ta beat the hell outta ya! You and your big flappin' jaw!" he snarled.

"Well, why don't ya? If you was to untie me—"

Immediately Clip was suspicious. "Oh, no, I ain't fallin' for that. Bull told me not to untie ya or let ya talk me into it, and I'm not gonna." He thrust his chin out aggressively.

"Did ya hear that, Jace?" Dave drawled. "His brother won't let him. That's why he won't fight me." Dave chuckled softly, and Clip got angrier.

"Now, now"—Jace felt it was his turn to put a few twigs onto the fire—"you can't blame Clip for using his brother as an excuse for avoiding a fight with you. You have such a terrible reputation, it's no wonder he's afraid."

"I ain't afraid!" Clip sputtered impotently.

Jace allowed a little smile to appear on his face. It made Clip all the madder.

"*I* know ya ain't hidin' beneath your brother's petticoats," Dave remarked laconically. "Better men than him—and I mean a lot better—have fled from a confrontation with Dave Merrill, Injun-whupper. Anyway, it just wouldn't be fair. I can see you're no fightin' man, Clip. I bet you don't even know how to wrastle. No, I don't mean no schoolyard wrastlin' betwixt boys," Dave added thoughtfully. "I mean backwoods wrastlin'.

I mean ranger wrastlin'. I can wrastle any man down in one minute flat. No one, save maybe the captain hisself, can take me down to the ground. That's a true fact, so I guess I can't blame ya none, Clip, for turnin' such a bright shade of yellow. You couldn't wrastle me iffen ya tried, and of course ya won't, 'cause your brother won't let ya."

Clip kicked the pot of coffee over with his foot, his fury warring with his common sense.

"Somethin' about that coffee disagree with ya, Clip?" Dave asked in a kindly manner.

"*You* disagree with me, Merrill, you and your big fat mouth!"

"Them are hard words for me to hear." Dave sounded hurt.

"Ya think I'm afraid? I ain't! I can beat ya wrastlin' any day of the week. With them weedy arms of yourn, it'd be easy! Have a look at this!" He yanked up a sleeve and showed off a thick, hairy arm plump with muscles. His hands were big with long, broad fingers.

Dave looked unimpressed. "Women's hands! My old granny has bigger arms!"

"That does it! This is the last time I'm gonna let ya make a fool outta me!" Flecks of foam gathered around Clip's mouth. His teeth looked large and square as he snarled in Dave's face. Dave got a gander at all of them. "I'll fight ya, and I'll beat ya. I'll shut that trap of yourn for good and all!" Clip pulled out his knife and cut Dave loose. "Now, ranger, what's your fightin' rules?" he rasped out. "Tell me now, afore I twist your neck into a knot!"

"That's better. Today you become a man, Clip. Well, all right then, Tuttle, if you're really serious." Dave rubbed his wrists until the blood flowed into them again. "First of all, get a big stick, and put it on the ground betwixt us," Dave ordered. Fuming, the big man took up the first piece of kindling he found and threw it to the ground. Dave frowned. "You'll need a bigger stick than that. You're a big man!"

"That's right, I am!" he shouted back, fetching a nice, thick piece.

"Here's the rules, Tuttle. Get down in a crouch. That's right. One of us on each side of the stick. At the count of five, come out a-grapplin'. And, listen, if either of us breaks the rules and makes a move afore the count of five, they get a free hit," Dave warned, wagging a finger at Clip.

"That sounds fair to me," Clip growled.

Both men got down into a crouch opposite each other, arms bent and ready. They glared hotly across that stick.

"Start countin', Tuttle."

"One . . ." Tuttle started to recite. Dave's hand swooped down, snatching up the heavy piece of wood. Before Tuttle could count to two, Dave had swatted Clip soundly across the head. The stick shattered, and Clip fell to the ground, unconscious.

Dave turned, grinning. "That's how rangers fight," he told Jace, picking up Clip's knife and cutting Jace free.

As Jace tossed the pieces of rawhide away, he saw Clip starting to stir. "Say, isn't Clip entitled to a free hit?" he reminded Dave dryly.

Dave looked abashed. "Why, you're right." He picked up another chunk of wood and whacked Clip over the head. He sank down again. "Don't you never say that Dave Merrill ain't a fair man." Dave shook a finger at Clip in reproof.

"We'd best get to Miss Prudence. We don't know what the others are doing to her," Jace said, already heading for his horse.

Dave flung himself into the saddle, and they headed out.

Chapter Thirteen

"Look out! It's the Tuttles!"

At the sudden explosion of galloping hooves, Riley was out of the cabin with his rifle up. Prudence flung herself out the door to stand at his shoulder and leveled her rifle at the big man riding the black horse.

"I'll take Bull!" she cried, firing as she spoke. The bullet tore at Bull's head and skimmed across his hairline.

"Put it down, Miss Prudence!" Bull yelled as he rode hard at her. He got there before she could reload. He pulled his horse to where she stood on the porch. "I've come back for ya," he said, laughing a brute's laugh, while she swung her empty rifle at him uselessly.

Frustrated tears filled her eyes, but she kept swatting at him. Getting nowhere, she dropped the rifle and ran for cover behind a water barrel. Bull's horse mounted the porch with a loud clatter of hooves across the planking. She jumped off the porch and ran along the pasture fence, then cowered in a narrow angle where two lengths of fence met. Tuttle followed relentlessly.

He urged his horse at her, pushing her back, farther back, against the rails, until there was no place for her to go.

"Why don't you just leave us alone!" she cried.

Bull threw his head back and roared. "You're gonna marry me, Miss Prudence! Ain't no two ways about it! I come here to claim my bride." His grin was evil. His horse moved again, pushing forward, crowding her. Prudence was a prisoner.

Riley couldn't help Prudence. He had his own predicament with which to contend. He had fired at Vole but missed his mark. Vole's horse had reached a dip in the undulating meadow, dropping its rider out of sight for that split second when Riley fired. He missed Vole, and he was flummoxed.

Dolly's mouth dropped open. "Ya missed him! I cain't hardly believe it!"

"Tremblin' timberdoodles!" Riley yelped. "Neither can I!"

Vole had ridden to one of the fences, leaned down, and tied a rope to the top rail. He nudged his horse, and the fence began to tear apart with the screech of splitting wood. The animals in the barnyard let up a wail. A calf bawled for its mother. The cries of scrambling, terror-stricken animals were deafening.

In the midst of it all Bull's voice rose up. "Pull it down, Vole! Pull it all down!" he ordered. Vole grinned and obeyed eagerly.

Seeing that grin fired Riley up. Full of anger, he took hold of his empty rifle and went running right at Vole. "Now you're askin' for grief!" he yelled.

"Send him to glory!" Dolly screeched.

Coming up behind Vole, Riley lashed the rifle's barrel across Vole's shoulder blades. The force of it tumbled Vole out of his saddle. He landed on his back, then sat up, eyes wide, trying to figure out how he'd gotten there. He stared up through the dust for the one who had knocked him down. He saw Riley, and his eyes narrowed into slits of hate.

Riley was winding up for another smack, but Vole ducked out of the way. His arm flung out at the rifle and struck it hard. It flew from Riley's hands. Vole's eyes commenced to gleam. His lips parted in a drooling smile while he stared at Riley's head. It reminded him of a gourd. He rose to his feet slowly. Keeping his eye on that head, he slapped crazily around his belt, feeling for one of his knives.

Riley looked into those wild eyes, spun around, and took off running. He skedaddled across the barnyard with the older, stronger boy hot after him. Around and around they went.

"I ain't afraid of ya! I ain't afraid of ya!" Riley yelled over his shoulder as he slipped and fell again and again, trying to keep just out of Vole's reach. "Don't think I am, 'cause I ain't!" Riley assured him in a high-pitched scream.

Vole bore down on him, excited by the chase. He almost caught hold of that boy—almost. Vole's long fingers jerked convulsively at the tempting sight of Riley's backside. This was better than a gourd—it was a-runnin'! Giggling, he kicked out at the new patch on Riley's britches.

After the first kick, Riley took a flying leap over a hay bale to avoid that eager foot. "You'll be sorry for that, Vole!" he gasped. Riley stopped for a moment to toss an empty pail in Vole's path, then kept going.

Dolly was busy too, whacking at Bull with the broom while he cursed at her hair and her freckles. A quick look showed Vole raising a knife to hurl at Riley's helpless back. That's when Dolly dropped the broom and grabbed a fistful of stones instead. She took off after Vole, her skirts flying. She cried out as Vole's knife sailed ahead, and the blade skimmed a groove along Riley's upper arm. Riley yelped with pain.

Dolly turned into a fury. Her freckles stood out. "Well, are ya crazy or somethin', Vole Tuttle? Don't ya know that that thar's his shootin' arm?" she shrieked at him. Soon she was right there on his heels, flinging those nasty little rocks with precision. She smacked

Vole in the back of the head and legs, the rocks stinging and whipping his flesh. They hurt so much that he
howled with pain. She had a mighty accurate aim.

"Dang ya!" he yelled. "Dang ya!" Then he gave
up chasing Riley. He stopped dead in his tracks and
turned to face Dolly, who skidded to a halt. They were
only a few feet apart now. A wrathful look filled his
face to overflowing as he pulled out his favorite skinning knife. Dolly's eyes bulged out as he moved the
blade in lazy, intimidating circles.

"Now, little girl, I'm gonna peel off all your freckles one at a time." His eyes glinted madly as he came
at her.

"Help!" Dolly hollered, turning to run. She charged
up the grassy hill away from the farm and into the trees.
Dodging over tree trunks and stumps, she slammed back
branches that stung Vole's face. Her short legs managed
to stay just ahead of the swishing knife.

Riley heard her call and took up the chase. In a few
bounding strides he was right behind Vole. He shot
forward. When he was close enough, he stretched his
body, diving through the air and landing on his stomach. He was able to snatch hold of one of Vole's ankles. Trying to kick free of the boy, Vole's legs got
tangled up. He stumbled erratically across brambles
and shattered tree limbs, still swinging his blade. Seeing Dolly's tantalizing apron so near, he lunged,
tripped, and sprawled forward with a heavy thump.
There he lay flat on his face without moving.

Dolly and Riley stopped running. They came back to him and watched for a moment. He still didn't move. They suspected a trick and stood together, Riley with his rifle and she with her hands full of stones. Nothing happened.

"Come on, Vole, I'll whup ya, ya coward. Pickin' on a defenseless girl!" Still nothing happened. "Don't ya play possum with me, boy. I'm a sight smarter than that!" Riley picked up a stick and gave the inert Vole a poke.

"I think we killt him," Dolly said starkly. "Look!" She pointed to some blood seeping onto a patch of bright leaves. "His life is a-drainin' outta him!"

Riley stepped closer. He pushed over the body. Dolly was right. " 'Pears he fell on his own knife." The halcyon days of Vole's frolicsome youth had clearly come to an end. He was dead, all right, with his favorite knife stuck between his ribs right up to the hilt, that empty grin still plastered on his face. Too late, Vole Tuttle had learned that a blade can cut both ways. Alas, it was a lesson to be learned only once.

"I reckon it'll be consolation to some that it was his favorite knife he fell on." They stood and stared at what they had done. Prudence's shriek brought them up sharp. "Let's take care of Bull now!" Riley shouted, and they turned and raced through the forest back to the farm.

They were heading to the porch to reload their rifles. That's when they heard it and stopped short.

They looked at each other with wonder. Riley hoped, and Dolly feared. Both waited, struck silent.

From beyond the trees it came: a rumbling sound in the earth. It was a sound Riley knew. It was the pounding of horses galloping nearer and nearer. Riley's heart swelled. It was either more enemies—or it was help.

Then he saw it.

One white horse, beautiful and majestic, sailed through the trees and onto the long slope. Riley had never seen it before. But on its back . . . Riley squinted, then cheered and cried with relief. "Jace!" he yelled. "Miss Prudence, it's Jace! I knowed Jace wouldn't let hisself be killt!" The tears ran down his tough face in dirty streaks.

And behind Jace was the legend himself. "Look! Look-see who be yonder!" For a while there Riley's hard little shell had been close to cracking. Now Riley grabbed Dolly's hands and danced around the yard with her. "Dave Merrill, the great Injun-whupper!" he sang out. "We're okay now!"

Bull heard it. It cut through his own laughter, and his smile was slapped away at the hearing of the news. He shot his head sideways to look, a murderous brooding commanding his features now. He swore hoarsely. His granite jaw clamped so tightly that the cuss words couldn't spew out fast enough.

Still, he doubted Riley. That boy was a natural-born liar, as he could testify. Suspecting a trick, Bull pulled his horse away from Prudence and stepped down from the saddle to find out what, exactly, was going on. He circled around the horse and grabbed Prudence by the upper arm—just in case—shoving her ahead of him. He dragged her around to the porch and waited for the horsemen to approach.

Doubt lingered long enough for him to recognize the white stallion and the man riding it. His jaw fell open. He knew, then, what had happened. "That blockhead, Clip!" he rasped out. "And where the hell's Vole?" he asked himself, his eyes searching the place. "Vole!" There was no reply.

The horsemen approached. It was Jace Cutter and Dave Merrill. They reined in in a blaze of fury.

"So!" he called out to them. "Ya got loose, huh? Well, I ain't Clip. I'm a heap more than he is. Ya think you can take me, do ya? For this?" He shook Prudence hard. "Is this what ya want to die for? 'Cause ya will! This bit of calico?" he taunted Jace.

Bull barely got the words out of his mouth when Jace leaped from the saddle and flew at Bull Tuttle's head. Jace was a big man, and his weight carried Tuttle to the grass. Yes, this was what he had faced the Shawnee for. This was what he was willing to die for. And the fight was on!

Bull was startled, but he hit the ground grappling. The two men commenced to batter each other, throwing hammer-strong punches.

Tuttle's horse stamped nervously, then galloped off,

while Dave came out of the saddle to pull a white-faced Prudence away from the fight.

"He's alive." The words barely whispered past her numb lips.

"Yes, ma'am," Dave assured her. Then he encouraged his friend. "Get it done with, Jace!"

The men rolled over and over, kicking up clods of earth. Grunting and swearing, each man tried to find an opening—an unprotected face, an ear to bite into, ribs to bash. Jace was ready to fight as dirty as Bull did. Jace's elbow buckled, then jolted straight out in one smooth motion, force-feeding a ball of angry knuckles into Bull's big mouth. Bull took it, damn him!

Jace struggled to pry his tough but more compact body out from under Tuttle's huge weight. The man was crushing his ribs. He gave a mighty heave. Rolling on top now, Jace landed punches—solid ones—with everything he had, into Bull's face and gut. His fingers got tangled in Bull's torn shirt, and he ripped it out of the way, baring Bull's torso. Tuttle's neck looked like a barrel; his chest, a wagonload of meat. An army could feed off him for a week. Jace dug into the pile of muscle underneath him, his fists drilling holes into Bull's gut.

Snarling, Tuttle tossed him off. He climbed rapidly to his feet, and Jace rose too.

Jace wiped the red spill from a scalp cut that dribbled into his eye. He grinned without humor. "I'm gonna take you apart, you big side of beef!"

Tuttle responded by swearing and knocking dirt and twigs from his pants. With a roar that started somewhere in his cavernous rib cage, he pulled his chin down. With an eye full of meanness, he came at Jace.

"Eat him up for supper, Jace!" Dave shouted encouragingly.

Jace was waiting with fists eagerly cocked. He stood there, unafraid of Tuttle's best hits. As Tuttle stepped up, he proceeded to rip into Bull's granite flesh. Right, left, jab, hook, and a right cross. First one, then another, then in combinations. He drove home his fists with all the hate and power stored up in him. He slammed Bull so fiercely that he felt the punches jolt up and down his own body.

"That'll learn him!" Dave wagged his head.

Filled with the desire to hurt him back for everything he had done to Prudence, Jace shot an uppercut that blasted Bull's chin and set his head askew. Tuttle gave it back with plenty extra. Jace's rage-driven fists wracked Tuttle's head and body, his quick, springlike jabs working over Tuttle's face. But Jace couldn't keep up the hectic pace for long. The spirit to maim was still alive, but he was becoming arm-weary. His strength began to flag. It was just what Bull was waiting for. When it happened, Bull stepped up.

"Now I'm done playin' with you, Cutter!" he barked,

rubbing a paw over his sore chin. Suddenly he slammed Jace in the stomach. Jace doubled over and lost color. He stood there while Bull struck him now with hard, walloping fists.

"Ya got him runnin' scared!" Dave flung out.

Jace's knees were starting to collapse. His head was whirling. Wisely, he backed off to catch his breath.

Bull turned from him with a disdainful grin. Now he wanted to take a hunk outta that Talking Otter. If it weren't for him, Bull knew, Clip wouldn't have been fooled into untying them.

Bull shifted his ill-natured gaze to Dave. "Now, flannel-mouth"—Bull crooked a finger at Dave— "you're next. I'm gettin' tired of your yappin'. I'm gonna yank out your tongue and make ya eat the danged thing!" He stomped over to Dave and swung a powerful right jab to where Dave lovingly stored the aforementioned appendage. Dave just managed to jerk his jaw to the side as the fist whizzed past his head in full flight.

Then Dave stepped in quickly and threw an upper-cut that would have felled most men he knew, yet Tuttle merely shrugged it off.

"Ya may be an Injun-whupper, but you're no Tuttle-whupper! C'mon, ranger, give it your best shot!" Bull invited, his hands hanging at his sides. He stuck out his chin to give Dave a clear shot. Gleefully, Dave took it. The wicked slug fell on Bull's chin like rain on a stone. Bull grinned a bloody grin. "I got a jaw of iron, ranger," he bragged.

Jace had gotten a second wind. He now leaped onto Tuttle's back. "Yeah, *pig* iron!"

Dave also saw the opportunity and laid into him.

"Show him how a ranger fights!" Riley called out to Dave.

With Jace clinging to his back, Tuttle used one big open hand to push Dave in the muzzle. Dave stutter-stepped backward to fall over his own feet and land in the dirt. Then Tuttle shrugged his beefy shoulders, spun nimbly around, and knocked Jace off. He took hold of Jace's throat with his thick fingers. He squeezed, and Jace gurgled.

"Don't let him git away, Jace!" Dave yelled. "Hold him for me. I ain't finished with him yet!"

Dave sprang to his feet, pushed up his sleeves, and rammed Tuttle. Bull had to drop Jace. Jace fell to the ground, gasping for air.

Then Dave took his place and threw every fighting technique he knew at the big keg of a man. He drove home his fists with zeal. Any trick he could think of, he tried: hooking, tripping, kicking, head-butting. After a while he was cheered to see that he had drawn blood, and not just his own.

"This reminds me of the time I was but ten years old, and this big Mohawk tried to whup me—" Without warning, Bull reached through Dave's fists and struck him smack in the face. The fond reminiscences ceased as Dave mopped up his blood. Bull beat him again and again till his head felt like wool. Breathing heavily, Dave swayed before Bull.

"Stop talkin' and start fightin', flap-jaw! You boys are borin' me!" He stalked to Dave and lifted him by the seat of his britches and the scruff of his neck. "This is what most people feel like doin' to ya!" With a tremendous heave, he tossed Dave through the air, aiming for the horse trough. Dave landed next to it, coming down with a loud bang on the hard-packed earth. Everyone gasped. Dave lay motionless for a heart-stopping second; then, slowly, he staggered to his feet. Everyone cheered.

Relieved, Riley yelled out tauntingly, "That was pretty bad throwin', Bull! Ya missed the outhouse by a mile! Why don't ya try again? Why don't ya?"

Dave backed off hurriedly. When his eyes cleared, he croaked. "Go on, Jace, I softened him up for ya."

Then Dave did the unexpected. While Tuttle snickered and turned to meet Jace's attack, he blindsided Bull with a kick to the chin. "I got real powerful legs, ya know!" Dave shouted. Tuttle fell back, shaken. He had no time to brace himself for the hit or duck out of the way. Dave's foot struck like a rock. It was damaging, all right. The agonizing pain took up his whole head.

Riley made a move to dive in and lend a hand, but Miss Prudence grabbed him and hugged him to her. "No, Riley, let the men handle this."

Through the buzz in his head Jace heard her words and saw her face beaming with pride. Feisty but plainly done in, Jace elbowed Dave aside. Dave allowed it. Prudence was Jace's woman. It was only fitting that he should have some of the glory.

"He's mine," Jace raked out, his voice gravelly in his throat. He moved in for what he realized was the last time. It was now or never. Anything left in his wearying body he marshalled into his fists. He tore into Bull with muscles churning. His blood surged hotly in his head and pounded in his ears like a thousand devils striking on anvils. If it killed him, he would stand there and take Bull down to his knees. For once, Bull Tuttle would get what he deserved.

"Thataway!" Riley shouted.

He kept at it. His arms swung like thrashing scythes. He didn't even realize when Bull finally stopped hitting and sank to his knees in exhaustion. Blood was in Jace's eyes, and he could only see red. He kept slugging into flesh, mashing into the pulp that once was a face. Bull went down hard on his backside, his head slipping onto his heaving chest.

"That's enough, Jace. Ya got him."

Jace was numb to the blows he was throwing. Dave had to grab his swinging fists in order to stop him. Right now he was just swinging at air. Tuttle was down. "Ya got him. It's done for, good and all."

Everyone was clapping. The fight was over. Prudence was at Jace's side, crying as she tenderly wiped the blood from his face. She led him to the porch, and Dolly came over with a basin of clean water. With gentle fingers Prudence tended his wounds.

Dolly patted his hand comfortingly. "There, there," Dolly cooed, "there, there."

Dave observed all this benignly through his battered eyes. "Ya did mighty good, Jace, for a beginner."

"He was wonderful!" Prudence's lips trembled, and her eyes were warm with love. It was there plain for Jace to see. "Oh, Jace!" Her voice quavered. "Bull told us you were taken by the Shawnee. I was out of my mind with worry."

"I was taken," he affirmed grimly, clasping her fluttering hands.

"Oh, no! How did you get away?" Dolly wanted to know.

"Well, it was like this, missy," Dave began, stepping forward. "I seen Jace tied up backward on that horse, a noose around his neck so tight, his eyes was bulgin' out bad and his face a-turnin' purple. So I—"

"We can talk about that later." Jace's voice sliced through Dave's words as he saw Prudence's horrified expression.

"That's right, ma'am. The main thing bein' I saved him, and with considerable trouble to myself."

Jace stood up with his arm still around Prudence while Dolly clung to his pants leg. "We should be leaving, shouldn't we, Dave?"

"You're plumb right. Why don't ya go get some food together, ma'am, along with all your weapons. We're gonna need 'em. Riley, go chase them cows up into the woods. They'll be safe there till we can come back to get 'em."

Prudence looked bewildered. "But why should we leave? Now that Mr. Tuttle"—she tried not to look at him—"has been taken care of."

"There's more than Tuttles in this here world, Miss Prudence," Dave interrupted. "There's them Shawnee. I don't mind confidin' to ya that they're all pretty near mad enough to chew their own moccasins since we escaped from 'em. Their hearts was set on us, and we eluded their hospitality."

"What do we do about Tuttle?" Jace asked, nodding to the man who was just coming to.

"I been thinkin' on Bull Tuttle. He could surely do with a little more readin'. Shakespeare, maybe. Keep him outta trouble." Dave shook his head. "Ya know, Jace, I'm right ashamed to get beat by someone so ignorant."

"What do we do with him now?" Jace asked patiently.

"Dolly Dooley!" Dave called. Dolly jumped up. "Throw some water over Bull afore he wakes up."

Dolly eagerly did his bidding, tossing the pail of cold well water over Bull, and the wooden pail after it. It struck him on the forehead as he struggled to get up. He cussed out the little girl.

"Should we take him in?" Jace asked Dave, pulling away from Prudence and picking up a piece of rope.

"Now, Jace"—Dave lowered his voice—"we ain't in no position to bring Tuttle in. There's still too much playfulness in him, and I ain't riskin' my hide to save his or his kin's. Them Shawnee are south of here. I'm a-thinkin' that maybe we could give this miscreant a second chance. We'll send him south—to freedom. Then we'll head north to the fort. What do ya say?"

"That sounds like a fine idea to me."

Dave swaggered to Bull, who still sat on the ground. Dave held a loaded rifle.

"So ya whupped me." Bull spat out a mouthful of blood. "Now what?"

"Tuttle, ain't no doubt you're one hell of a fightin' man. But you was wrong to try to force Miss Dooley to marry ya. I know she's pretty and all, but it was plumb wrong. But that's not the only thing. Ya also stole land from other settlers. The good thing—the only good thing—is that ya ain't killed anyone yet that we know about, so we're gonna give ya another chance to start over elsewhere. Start walkin' south, and we'll say no more about it. This is no place for ya here, nor none of your kin. 'Cause iffen ya don't skedaddle, Captain Maxcy will be after ya with a full contingent of rangers. Best leave now while the gettin's good. You can pick up Clip at your own camp."

Bull got shakily to his feet.

"And if ya take some advice, Bull, read yourself some Shakespeare. That's all I got to say."

Bull gave them a long look. "Where's Vole?"

Dolly spoke up. "He's yonder, under the trees. He fell on his knife whilst a-chasin' me."

Bull turned without a word and went to collect Vole. With Vole's body slung over his shoulder, he rounded up his horses and left. All spirit seemed to have deserted him.

"There goes a changed man," Dave predicted.

When Riley came back, they all saddled up and departed. They headed for Fort Pitt. And Angie Wright.

Chapter Fourteen

Dave pulled up when he heard Riley calling out behind him.

"Mr. Dave Merrill, sir!" Riley saluted smartly. "Injuns comin' up. More than twenty of the beggars!"

"How close are they?" Dave looked thoughtful.

"A few more minutes and they'll be a-peckin' at our heels! They're comin' along faster than relations headin' for their Sunday supper."

"I shoulda knowed they wouldn't be sidetracked by them worthless Tuttles." Dave sounded disgusted as he saw his simple plan fall apart. He should have realized that such a great personage as himself—Dave Merrill, Indian-whipper—was bound to be more interesting to them savages. "I shoulda knowed I couldn't escape my fame." He sighed philosophically. "Well, let's snap it

214

up, then. There's a place up here that I've been havin' in
my mind. Come here, boy." Riley brought his horse up
alongside Dave. "I got a big job for ya—a job for a
man. Can ya do it?"

"Yes, I can!" the boy replied, straightening his shoulders. "And proud to!"

"Good. Now, you and Jace, here, are gonna take
the ladies to safety—back to Fort Pitt. Jace knows the
way."

Jace's lips tightened; already he didn't like Dave's
plan. "And what are you going to do while I'm leading
everyone to safety?" he rasped out.

"Now, that's somethin' betwixt me and myself. You
just do what I say. That's an order," Dave drawled maddeningly.

"I'm not in the Army, and I'm not letting you face
them Injuns alone." Jace was stubborn.

"Jace has a point there, Mr. Dave Merrill, sir," Riley
interrupted anxiously.

"Dang blast the both of ya!" Dave erupted. "I got me
a plan, see, and you're a-ruinin' it. Lookee here." He
was leading them as he talked. The three were soon
looking at a clearing of uneven ground surrounded by a
thick, curving ledge the shape of a horseshoe. Jace
could see the advantage of having the Indians caught in
the semicircle, where they could be enfiladed by rifle
fire.

"They're gonna be surrounded and ambushed," Dave
pointed out craftily.

"With one rifle?" Jace's tone was skeptical.

"Dave Merrill's rifle, that bein' the difference. Now you git along there. Wait up!" Dave slipped out of his new jacket and shirt. Handing them to Jace, he said, "Hold on to these. Them's my courtin' clothes. I'm gonna need 'em again iffen I live through this." For the first time his eyes met Jace's, and they were troubled. "Now you tell Angie—" He stopped. "Tell her—" He groped for words.

Jace took the jacket and shirt and put them into his saddlebag. "I'll tell her. And I'll be back as soon as the girls are safe."

"I appreciate knowin' ya, Jace."

The men shook hands, and then Jace took the women up the incline. Dave waited below. When they reached the woods, Jace pulled up his horse.

"Riley, you take the ladies to the fort." Prudence turned and stared at him, tears forming in her eyes. "I love you, Prudence." He reached out one arm and pulled her closer. He kissed her warmly. "But I'm not the kind of man to desert a friend. Even if he is Dave Merrill, Injun-whupper." A small, sad smile curved his lips. He gave the sign to Riley, and Riley urged the girls forward.

"Come along, ma'am, Miss Dolly Dooley. Don't want to be where the gunfire is. Ya got nothin' to worry about. Dave and Jace'll take care of them savages easy." Riley threw a worried look over his shoulder as Jace disappeared.

After tying up his horse, Jace took his rifle and positioned himself behind some logs with a good view of any oncoming warriors. He was about to call to Dave to let him know he was there, when the words died a short death in his throat.

Out of the dark woods the Indians began to pour. They came with only a whisper of sound, their eyes on the tracks that Dave had not bothered to disguise. Some were suspicious, some were eager; all were careful as their horses minced at the fringes of the woods. They looked over the situation with foreboding. They didn't like it. Their eyes took in the tall, curving ridge studded thickly with trees and scrub. A thousand guns could be hidden there. *Too bad,* the thought went through Jace's mind, *there were only two.*

Dave crouched behind a huge rock and waited. It was one of several scattered about the place, but the only one large enough for a person to hide behind. Through the bushes that surrounded him, he could see the Indians studying the ground. Five sets of hoofprints they would be counting, and so they must figure that five guns were around here someplace. Their eyes lifted to the horseshoe-shaped ridge. For a long moment they searched the trees and thought. Dave let them think for a while. He knew they'd be thinking and wondering if finding He-Who-Cannot-Be-Caught was worth the risk. He saw their nasty little eyes examine the rock behind which he waited. No one seemed very eager to

come over and look behind it. It was as if they sensed
another presence. For a while they waited—and waited
some more.

There was one buck Dave figured to be that pretty
bird Jace had spoken of. He was a good-looking fella
with a big sneer on his face. His chest was sticking out
proudly, as if daring someone to shoot into it. He
didn't come near the rock, though. Dave watched that
sneer. No one came near that rock.

When nothing happened, the Indians began to talk
among themselves, as Dave figured they would. It was
time for everyone to give his opinion, and each gave
it loudly. Preening Bird was the most emphatic. He
pointed to the horseshoe-shaped ledge and urged them
to move forward. That old Miami Dave had left atop
Timber Wolf Pass had words with him. All joined in,
taking sides. As the minutes passed with no enemy in
sight, Preening Bird became louder and more demand-
ing. He wanted immediate action. There seemed to be a
question as to who was in authority. Preening Bird was
trying to take control. The old Miami snarled back.
Now, in all this confusion, was the time to make a
move.

Dave Merrill stepped out into the open.

All talking ceased at once. All eyes flew to the lone
figure standing in front of them, seemingly indifferent
to his peril. All became still in that dark woods. Dave
stood there, tough as the old elms that surrounded
him, a rifle hanging down in one sinewy hand, the

other menacingly fondling the smooth wooden handle
of his 'hawk. Gritty and dangerous he was—every
leather-tough inch of him. His eyes, like the blue
sheen of steel, went slowly over them. He appeared to
be weighing them with cool effrontery. The eyes did
not even flicker at the number of warriors facing him.
The handsome face, set and somber, did not betray
uncertainty or fear. On the contrary, there was a reckless impudence in his gaze, a don't-give-a-damn glit-
ter that made the Indians leery. Surely the white man
must have more rifles behind him to stand there so audaciously alone, with only his meager weapons with
which to fight them.

Apprehensively the Indians' eyes probed the woods
beyond. Nothing moved. They seemed to be alone,
alone with He-Who-Cannot-Be-Caught. Distrust rode
them. Their gaze dwelled contemplatively on the inso-
lent smile that had crept onto Dave's face. There was
too much boldness evident, too much gall.

Dave took a step forward, and the warriors' eyes narrowed at once. He had picked up an object that lay
curled up like a serpent in a well of rocks next to him.
Dave held it up high, and the warriors caught their
breath. It was a long strand of bear claws! So this was
what had happened to their comrade! The old ones had
not taken him—the white man had! A furious chatter
ran through them.

Dave stood there, while the light brought out the
burnished copper in his hair. The deepening sun shone

on his tanned chest. The orange rays gleamed so brightly over him that, for an instant, Dave's bare torso resembled golden armor—the armor of a fighting man ready to launch himself into battle.

Dave drew back his arm and let fly the string of bear claws. Deliberately, challengingly, it landed in front of Preening Bird's horse.

The buck grunted, surprised and angry at being singled out. His horse shied from the sinister object. It was as if Bear Claw himself had been tossed contemptuously onto the ground. Scorn sat on Dave's rock-solid jaw. He waited for the challenge to be taken up.

Preening Bird didn't move.

Dave commenced to cuss them out in Shawnee. He cussed them, the whole kit and caboodle of their ancestors, and Bear Claw as well. Particularly Bear Claw. He even cussed out Preening Bird as he sat watching the white man with loathsome contempt. Dave spat on the ground.

"Uhhh!" Preening Bird's face contorted with anger. Feathers ruffled, he immediately slid from the saddle, outraged, war club in hand. He had had much luck with that war club and would have again, he figured. The white man had called him out, and he was glad—very glad—to oblige. The sooner someone dispatched him, the better.

Dave stood ready, his very soul blazing with the unquenchable fire of battle. He had the daring of a man with a vast army standing behind him. Yet he stood alone. He seemed oblivious as one of the other Indians, far to the back of the war party, crawled from his horse and crept along the rocky wall. What he had done to Jace Cutter, he would now do to Dave Merrill. The buck would come around behind Dave and kill him while Preening Bird kept him busy. The Indian hefted his 'hawk and picked his way, grinning.

Preening Bird, as if unaware of what the other Indian was doing, walked toward Dave with the same cold absorption with which he had walked toward Cutter just days ago. His eyes affixed to Dave's, he moved sinuously, like a snake winding through the grass. Closer he came to Dave, then closer. He started to slap his war club in his palm. Although the others watched the happenings with fascination, they were still wary. Surely this must be a trap. He-Who-Cannot-Be-Caught just stood there, unafraid. The blue eyes glinted. The Indians did not know if it was with devilry or insanity. All waited to see what Preening Bird would do and how he would fare.

Spellbinding as Preening Bird was, Dave was not enthralled. His eyes narrowed when he caught a movement off to his right. He knew exactly what was happening. Instantly he swung up his rifle, snapped it sideways, and fired into the body of the other brave who was silently running at Dave to topple him with his 'hawk. The warrior's face looked surprised as he dropped to the ground. After a while he painfully crawled away, too hurt to finish the attack.

Dave was still reloading when Preening Bird came rushing at him. Another rifle rang out as Dave slammed his own to his shoulder. Preening Bird stumbled clumsily. It was the first clumsy move he had made. Blood pouring from his side, he flapped through the clearing like a big, awkward turkey, now ugly and plucked bare of his wonderful plumage and majestic manner. He crumpled to his knees before his enemy and fell, beak first, into the dirt.

A wonderful smile lit up Dave's face as he realized someone else had made that shot. Jace, of course. Good old Jace!

The Indians looked on as their beautiful warrior, the pride of the Shawnee war chiefs, fell dead. It was bad medicine! Once again He-Who-Cannot-Be-Caught had killed one of their magnificent ones. No wonder the ancestors were enraged with them. They were enraged with them for allowing the white man to taint their realm with his evil presence and his black magic.

On the heels of this shock came the realization that the bullet had not come from Dave's rifle. It had come from above—in the woods. The old Miami's gaze swiveled from the woods to Dave. Dave stood with his rifle loaded, his face devoid of expression. If the shot from above came as a surprise to him, he didn't betray it.

Other sounds began to sift down to the waiting warriors: creeping noises, rustling noises, whispering noises. The place seemed alive with something unseen.

It was all around them. They began to fear that He-Who-Cannot-Be-Caught's ancestors were now lying in wait for them. The ridges of the old Miami's face hardened as he rejected the notion. He knew the ancient forerunners of his tribe were stronger. After all, didn't they hold Timber Wolf Pass as their own?

The white man's composure angered him. The old Miami wanted to teach him a lesson. He couldn't allow him to rob the ancestors of their most valiant and glorious warriors without paying for this crime. He lifted his rifle and took meticulous aim. Instantly Jace's rifle boomed again. The concussive noise split the air wide open. The old Miami felt blood run down his arm. Dave stood unharmed. Another rifle boomed, and another, as the Indians, following their chief's lead, dug their heels into their horses and began to charge.

Gun smoke swirled around from the dark stand of trees. The old Miami looked up and stared in disbelief as the once-silent forest began to give up its inhabitants.

A big black stallion plunged out of the woods, dark and daunting. Atop him, the rider, his features chiseled like gray granite, was frighteningly familiar.

"Maxcy!" someone whispered. Head of the rangers!

Another horseman appeared next to him. It was Jean Laurier, the Frenchman. It was said that his fists were even more deadly than his knife. Others appeared, faster and faster, filling the horseshoe-shaped arena. The Indians knew it was a losing battle. Regretfully, bitterly, the old Miami gave the sign to get the hell out of there. They wheeled their ponies and charged back out, fighting each other to be first up the trail.

Before he left, the old Miami's black eyes nailed into Dave. "The stone kings are hungry to avenge the warriors of their blood! He-Who-Cannot-Be-Caught may yet have his hide stripped from his bones! The old ones will not be mocked!" He urged his horse, and then he was gone, the horse flying over the ground amid spitting bullets.

The ranger corps took after them. In the devastating chaos, seven bucks lay dead. The live ones were harassed as they retreated all the way back to the banks of the river. By the time the rangers returned, Riley and the Dooleys had made their way back.

"I told ya Jace and Dave would take care of all them savages," Riley told the girls heartily.

Prudence leaped off her horse and went to hug Jace. Dolly wept on his leg. The rangers all came to greet him.

"Danged if I didn't even know you was a-missin'," Nash Winslow exclaimed, belting Jace on the back in a congratulatory manner.

"How did you get mixed up with Dave Merrill?" Sam Logan wanted to know.

Jace explained briefly how he had been caught and how Dave had rescued him.

"A burnin' skull!" Sam's voice was amazed. "I'd like to hear the story about that one!"

"You will," Jace predicted. "I have to admit,

though"—Jace became serious—"if Dave hadn't found me, I'd be dead. I owe him my life."

"I won't never throw rocks at him!" Dolly promised fervently.

"I knowed he was great. I just didn't know how great." Riley was awed.

Maxcy reined in. "Dave! Am I glad to see you in one piece! I thought for sure those old gods up top of Timber Wolf Pass had fried your bacon into cracklings by now!" Maxcy dismounted and gave his friend an enthusiastic hug.

"Dave Merrill's too tough a proposition for them to chaw on," he commented. "But, Tom"—he showed a worried expression not often seen on the confident face—"did Angie, er, Mrs. Wright—get to the fort all-right?" Anxiety stood out starkly on him. His voice was strained.

Maxcy hid a smile. "Well, that depends on what you mean by 'allright.' She was cryin' and wailin' that you were caught by the Indians, and she begged us to come save you."

Dave's smile was wide and gratified. "Cryin', too?"

"Yep. You'd think she'd lost a twenty-dollar gold watch, the way she was carrying on. She seemed to think you were worth something, I reckon. Probably believes you're dead and gone by now. We all thought it. Had a mighty fine wake for you too. Pity you weren't there." By now, all of Dave's friends were gathering around him, exclaiming happily at finding him alive.

"By golly, boy, you're still on this side of paradise!" Nash Winslow was astounded. "Thought for sure we'd be haulin' your heart-rendin' remains to the fort to be buried. Had a place picked out for ya already. Nice place."

"Dave!" Sam Logan elbowed his way over with Duke Jordan. They were both ecstatic to find Merrill in one piece. "You coulda knocked me over with a suet puddin' when I seen ya there a-wavin' them damned bear claws in the air! Here they are." Sam handed them to Dave. He had found them where they lay in the dirt.

Dave took them and stowed them carefully away. "Mayhap I'll tell ya the fabulous tale of how I got them, one of these fine old days. But right now I'd rather eat. Them savages sure don't feed their guests much of nothin'."

The men went about getting a camp going right in the center of the ledges. After they ate, they would make straight for the fort. For now, they all needed some coffee and food.

Jace took a bundle from his horse. "Dave! Here's your, ahem, courtin' clothes," Jace said loudly, handing them to Dave. There was a complete silence. Everyone stopped what he was doing to stare, open-mouthed, at Dave.

Blushing furiously but keeping his exterior calm, Dave nonchalantly took the items. "Thank you, Jace. Reckon I'll put them on." Dave's eyes flickered around at all of the men. Finally they honed in on Tom

Maxcy, who was grinning widely. Slowly Dave strolled up to him. He held up his shirt, then jammed his arms into the sleeves, holding Maxcy's guileless look with a stiff-lipped one of his own.

"Reckon I'll be puttin' them on. No one objectin'?" Dave's voice was challenging, as if daring Maxcy to tease him.

"Nice shirt," Tom said innocuously, managing to swallow down a thousand little amusing remarks that came to mind. Dave didn't seem in a mood for them.

"'Tis a nice shirt, and a nice coat." Dave's voice was bellicose.

"And ya look right smart a-standin' in 'em," Monty added with admiration.

Dave seemed appeased. "Thank ya, Monty. Well said."

Sam Logan had less self-control than Maxcy. "You goin' courtin'?" he asked eagerly.

"Well, maybe I will, and maybe I won't. Leastways, you ain't gonna be the first to find out. And you there!"—he pointed to the rest of the men—"can all go back to what you was doin' afore Sam asked that thought-provokin' question that gives rise to impertinent speculation and idle talk. 'Cause I ain't barin' my manly soul to any of ya!"

"The widda sure is a fine woman," Nash Winslow remarked appreciatively. "Why, if I was five years younger, I'd dance her to the altar."

"Five years?" Dave was insulted. "Make it fifty."

"Well, if you're gonna be affrontin' my dignity that-away, I'll make it ten! But no more, no matter how much ya push me," Nash declared.

Jean Laurier intervened. "Madame Wright is a person most lovely." He came up and brushed some dust off Dave's shirt collar. "Any man would be lucky to win her. But she does not want any man. No. She does not even want the best man. She wants Dave Merrill!" He winked.

Dave took a deep, relieved breath. "You been speakin' the truth there. She's a—wait a minute! Did you go slippin' an insult in there?"

"I do not notice. I speak from the heart," Jean said simply.

"Well, all right, then." Dave was mollified. "But what I do after I put on these here clothes is no one's business but mine. So I'll thank ya kindly to stop your cluckin' and get about your jobs." The men went back to what they were doing, but they still whispered excitedly about Dave.

"Too bad ya didn't meet Prudence first." Dolly came up to Dave and smiled. "You're not so bad."

"Thank you, young whippersnapper, but I already got me—" He stopped as Jace's eyes turned knowing. "Things to do," he finished up coolly. "Why don't ya go take Monty's bread? He ain't a-lookin'." Dolly agreed and hurried off. "You sure you want to marry Prudence Dooley?" Dave asked Jace in a low whisper.

She was off a ways talking to Maxcy. Seeing the two men looking at her, she smiled and waved shyly.

"I am," Jace said fervently.

"You'll have to take that little raspberry with her," Dave warned with a grin.

"She's a nice girl," Jace assured him.

"I guess she might be if ya feed her regular," Dave conceded, his smile turning to a soft laugh. "She sure is an eatin' girl." He, too, had experienced Dolly's propensity to snitch food from another's plate.

"By the way," Jace said casually, "I owe you for saving my life."

Dave shrugged. "A man helps his friends. That's what he's here for."

"I'd like to make something for you to give to Angie," Jace stated, watching his reaction. Dave's face stilled. "A necklace or a brooch. Something to memorialize the great occasion of your saving her life," Jace went on smoothly.

Dave was suddenly busy with his coffee. "That's right decent of ya. And I thank ya for it—for Angie, ya see? I'd like to give her somethin' pretty," he added wistfully.

"Consider it done," Jace remarked, keeping his tone serious. "I'll start on it as soon as we get to the fort."

Dave perked up at the thought. At last, he had something to give Angie for a change. Dave drank his last cup down with a grin. He wanted the gift to be pretty, real pretty! Like her. And it was a fair exchange, he told himself. Hadn't he saved Jace's life?

When they packed up to leave, he exceeded himself in high spirits. Soon he would see Angie again. He hadn't seen her since—Dave remembered the kiss. It burned in his memory. He turned red even while he rode along. Such audacity! Had she liked it, or hadn't she? The question tormented him.

His high spirits took a bit of a plummet as he wrestled with the answer. Then a new fear took hold of him. He got to thinking about all the mean, pesky little things he had said about the institution of marriage. He flinched with mortification at his many smirks and witty remarks at Angie's expense.

Dave worried all the way to the fort. When it finally came into view, he stretched his neck to see inside the gates. There was quite a crowd. One of the rangers had ridden on ahead to tell everyone the good news. Dave, for once, disregarded the crowd. There was only one person he wanted to see—only one person to whom he wanted to speak. He wanted to see Angie. His brow creased into an agitated frown. He had to see her. He had to know. . . .

There was a great commotion by the gate. Penny Holt rushed to the window to peep out. "Angie!" She spun around and started to laugh happily. "It's the men! They've come home. And I see Dave! He's alive!"

Angie dropped her sewing and shakily pushed out

of her chair. Her eyes were locked on Penny's face, as if she were afraid to look elsewhere.

"Alive?" Her lips trembled around the word. Her voice expressed doubt and hope at the same time.

"There he is!" Penny waved toward the gate. "Still wearing his new coat and shirt, although," she admitted, still smiling, "a little worse for wear. Poor man! What he must have been through!"

Angie started crying, pulling her apron to her face to wipe away the tears. Hesitatingly, she ran to the window to look herself. There he was: battered and bloody but grinning his old grin. His eyes raked the crowd of faces eagerly, as if searching for someone. "He is alive!" There was wonder in her voice. "Oh, Penny, I was so afraid! I didn't dare to think about it!" Her voice was thick with tears. "He's alive." It came out as a whisper. With a deep sigh of pleasure and relief, she grabbed her shawl to wrap about her and hurried out the door with Penny.

Angie had eyes only for Dave Merrill. She didn't notice anyone else as she headed toward him. People saw her and nudged one another, but all Angie saw was Dave's dear face. It was bruised and cut, his right eye was blacked, and he limped—but he was alive! And he was back.

With a little cry of gladness, Angie flew across the hard ground to where the men were walking their horses. Everyone was crowding around, congratulating them and patting them on the back. By golly, Dave had done it. He had gotten away from them Indians once more. Was there ever such a man as he?

Angie came to an abrupt halt about twenty feet away, suddenly shy. What if—what if he didn't really want her? Then Dave stopped and saw Angie. She still wore her apron and was fiddling nervously with the skirt of her dress, but there was no mistaking the love shining in her eyes.

The whole fort stopped. Silence settled in, probably for the first time in that bustling place. The quiet crowd waited, mighty interested to see what would happen. They all knew about Dave and Angie. What would the unbridled, untamed Dave do? There was no denying he was a splendid but solitary man. Would he break the widow's heart? Would he spurn her in front of the entire fort?

Dave smiled and held his arms wide. It was the intense and passionate expression in his eyes that sent Angie running the last few steps to him. There was no doubt about it, Dave Merrill was in love! His arms tightened around her slim figure as she sobbed on his chest. Gently he patted her shiny hair. When her sobs lessened, he pulled her away and kissed her right in front of everybody. He didn't care who saw what. He did it again, just to make sure everybody knew what he was about.

The crowd started jabbering at once, but Dave was not finished. No, sir, not yet. He intended to do things properly and in front of everyone. Angie deserved that much, and so he would do it. With some difficulty he got down on one injured knee, not even noticing as the gravel cut painfully into it. The people saw and gasped into silence once more. Dave took Angie's hand in his and looked earnestly into her face.

Her face stilled as she realized the significance of the occasion.

"Miss Angie Wright, ma'am, I know I'm not worthy of your regard. I am a mere mortal a-standin' right here in the presence of an angel. But even knowin' that you're far above me, I'm still wantin' to marry ya. Yeah, ya heard me!" He looked around at the people who immediately began to chatter. "I want to marry Miss Angie Wright! And, Angie, I'd be the happiest man alive iffen ya was to consent to be my wife. I ain't got much to offer, but such as it is, it's yours." He stopped and looked at her anxiously. She was staring, but not from indecision, just from shock. Dave was proposing to her in front of the whole fort!

A small, sweet smile came to her lips, and she blushed. "Thank you, Dave Merrill, I would love to be your wife."

Dave managed to get quickly to his feet, despite the pain, and grabbed her once more, kissing her soundly. "I know I don't deserve ya, but I don't care! I'll do my best to make ya happy!"

"So He-Who-Cannot-Be-Caught has been caught at last!" Jean clapped him on the shoulder. Everyone started cheering. Dave turned red but put his arm around Angie's shoulders. "Why don't you get married right now?" Jean suggested slyly, expecting Dave to back down.

But Dave was more than willing. He'd had enough of wandering. A wife and home seemed like paradise to him. "That's a right good idea, if Miss Angie Wright don't mind." He looked down at her worriedly.

Angie was smiling widely. "I'd like that more than anything," she admitted shyly.

The whole crowd went wild. A wedding! And Dave Merrill's, at that! What a day this was. Everyone wanted to witness this incredible event.

"Then let the weddin' festivities commence!" Dave shouted.

"I'm surprised ya got the gumption left after all them Indians ya fought!" Monty called out, astounded.

"How many was it that chased you and Mrs. Wright again?" one old-timer asked wickedly, wondering what he'd say.

Dave's arm around Angie's waist, he turned to them. "Why, there must have been about twenty of them red devils, but I didn't mind none. It was just a regular day in the life of Dave Merrill." Then his words skidded to a halt, as he remembered at once that Angie had been there as well. She had known exactly how many Indians there were. He looked down at her hesitatingly. "Er, how many Injuns do ya reckon there was, Angie?" he asked slowly. "In all the excitement, I mighta miscalculated."

Angie looked at him and started to smile. "I don't think there were twenty," she began. A few men started to snicker at Dave's tall tale. Dave's face fell. "I think there were more like thirty," she insisted, wide-eyed. "Maybe even more," she added helpfully.

A huge grin spread over Dave's face. "By golly, you're the girl for me!" He hugged her to him. "Let's have that weddin'. The sooner the better!"

The whole crowd went with them to the minister to see the wondrous sight.

Angie had finally gotten her man!

Epilogue

Dave Merrill was frisky and ready for fun as he leaned against the counter at Ford's Trading Post. Marriage had not changed him except for giving him an even keener taste for adventure. At heart he was the same old lovable flap-jaw he had always been. Although happily busy on his new farm, he tried to take time, every now and then, to liven up Ford's by dispensing his tales. As a matter of fact, he had some new, fully ripe stories he was busting to test out on untried ears. His bright eyes skipped over the usual roomful of patrons, trying to decide who would benefit most from his wisdom, when he spied a stranger. He was a big brute of a man with wide shoulders, flowing dark hair, and a full beard.

"Who's he? That black-haired man?" Dave asked Ford. "Looks mighty colorful." Dave looked him over carefully.

The stranger sat by himself with a bottle and glass in front of him. He was dressed in buckskins that had seen much better days. His wide face looked fierce and wild.

"Some stranger just come in today. I'd let him be if I was you, Dave. He looks pretty salty." Ford read Dave's mind. "Been over the mountain and back again, I'd say."

"Bosh! Why, he looks like he still has his baby teeth, if ya can find them amongst all that shrubbery. Reckon I can stack up against any hunter," Dave bragged.

The man seemed fresh from the woods, and Dave just knew he'd be eager to both receive and provide entertainment. Dave's eyes acquired a sparkle; he was hellbent on doing his good deed for the day. He resolved that this here fortunate individual would be the recipient of his unbosomings.

"Reckon I'll go over and exchange some pleasantries. He looks like a man desirous of enlightenment. And I got plenty." He swaggered to the corner where the man sat.

"Afternoon, stranger. Name is Dave Merrill." He stuck out his hand in a friendly manner. The stranger looked at it, looked at Dave, then poured himself another drink. "Ya got yourself a name?" Dave asked, not a whit put out by his cool reception.

"Yep." The newcomer took a drink and smacked his lips over it. "I do." There was a long silence.

"Guess ya don't know who I am," Dave remarked, pulling out a chair and straddling it, arms resting on its back.

The man stopped with the drink halfway to his mouth. His eyes narrowed. He seemed displeased at Dave's presumption. After a long, hostile look he continued drinking.

Dave ignored the look. "I'm Dave Merrill." He spoke slowly and clearly. Obviously, by the man's lack of delight, he hadn't caught it the first time. "You probably heard of me?" Dave prompted.

The light, hard eyes looked back expressionlessly. "No. I haven't," he barked. He sounded as if he didn't want to.

"Ya haven't?" Dave was shocked. He recovered quickly. "That's 'cause you're new hereabouts. I'm just about the best dang Injun-fighter around here. The Injuns have a name for me. They call me He-Who-Cannot-Be-Caught!"

"You referrin' to Indians or women?" one of his friends at a nearby table interjected, laughing. Cold Eyes' expression didn't change.

"I'm a ranger, ya know, one of Captain Maxcy's." The man's head shot up as if he finally understood something. His frigid, blank eyes drilled into Dave's skull. They resembled bits of steel. Their intensity would have staggered a lesser man, but Dave didn't feel a thing. He continued on blithely.

"I'm known as one of his best, if not *the* best, barring the captain hisself, of course." Dave was all modesty. "Because in one day—listen to this!—in one day I killt me forty Injuns. Ya heard me a-right, mister—forty. I'll admit to takin' a rest in between. I'll give ya that. Fightin' Injuns is mighty tirin', you can take it from me. But that was all in one encounter. Forty Injuns. One encounter." Dave brought his hand down on the table and nodded. "True story."

The man stared back. He was not conspicuously impressed.

"Fact is," Dave continued, believing he had found himself a rapt audience, "we just come back from patrol today. Keepin' order and suchlike. Well, sir, we come upon this homestead that was under attack, ya see? They were givin' them settlers a mighty hard time of it. 'Course, once them Shawnee seen us a-comin', they hightailed it outta there. They was in such a hurry, they forgot to take their dead with 'em. Probably saw me a-comin'."

Dave continued. "Whilst I was goin' about the place settin' things to right, I come upon this Injun's carcass. You'd be considerably confounded iffen I was to tell ya where I found that carcass. So I'll tell ya and spare ya the apprehension. I found him under a cow. Unbelievable as that may sound to some, that's where

I found him." A light thrill of applause came from the audience as they showed their satisfaction. Dave bowed. "Yes sir, with all that commotion a-goin' on, that poor cow just collapsed. I seen them skinny legs stickin' out from underneath that old cow, and I knew there was plenty more there." Dave started to laugh. "Ya shoulda seen that Injun's face when we peeled that heifer off him. He sure died surprised!"

Several of Dave's friends guffawed. "Can you imagine what they're goin' to tell his widda? 'He died bravely: a cow fell on him.' Or maybe, 'Your husband met up with a cow, and the cow won.' They'll be tellin' that around the campfires for years to come!"

Dave evidently thought this was hilarious, because he laughed so much, tears came to his eyes. Everyone else in the place laughed long and loud as well. The stranger didn't even blink.

"Now, first ya gotta ask yourself what the odds are of that happening. I sure wouldn't take no bets! Haven't seen that writ on any headstones lately. Second, ya kind of wonder how a healthy man allowed a cow to just fall on him altogether. He musta been crouchin' behind her, thinkin' himself safe, when she plumb swooned upon him." Dave wiped away his tears of mirth with the back of one hand.

"Now, I can see a question hoverin' about your jowls." Dave leaned forward. "You're a-wonderin' what happened to that poor old cow. Well, I'm glad to tell ya that when we lifted her back up onto her toes, she was fine and dandy. Settin' on Injuns appeared to agree with her."

The frosty-eyed stranger took another drink and looked up at the ceiling. His face was carved of granite.

"And danged if that weren't a good story!" Dave confided to Ford as he left his chair and came to lean against the counter again, frustrated. "I've felt more warmth from a tombstone than from him. Corpses is friendlier."

"I wouldn't tangle with him, boy. Them quiet ones can be mighty mean. They got a lot of feelin's pent up inside them. Then one day, they can't take no more, and they just blow up. 'Specially them that don't see many people from one year's end to another. They ain't easy with people. Looks to me like he ain't seen nobody in a coon's age. Look at them light blue eyes starin' outta that bushy head like an owl's. And he's all tensed up, like he's ready to pounce on somebody."

"Well, it's time he became more sociable," Dave pondered out loud. "Bet I could out-wrastle him." He stroked his chin, looking the man up and down. "I'm as tall as he is."

"Don't you be thinkin' like that. I'd rather prod a bear than prod that one."

Dave seemed to think this was a reflection on his manhood. "He may be bigger, but I'm all muscle."

"So's he. Mark my word. Don't bait him, or you'll come to grief. I knew a man once'st. Quiet-like. Didn't say much. His partner was somethin' else. Talked like it was goin' out of style. One day this man gets plumb fed up with the talker and takes an axe to him."

Dave watched as Mrs. Ford put a plate of stew and some bread in front of the man. The man merely grunted.

"Ain't got him no manners at all."

"Takes an axe to him," Ford repeated.

"Think he'll take an axe to me?" Dave asked interestedly.

"Never know," Ford answered. "He's carryin' one, so stay out of swingin' range. And don't bother him whilst he's eatin'. Some men get all rageful when they're vexed right in the middle of their eatin'."

"Well, at least it'll be a change. The only thing I seen move on that moss-covered face is his eyes. They commence to bloat every time I talk."

"Well, if you look sharp, you'll see somethin' else moving. He's sure forkin' down them vittles."

"Danged fast too." Dave stopped. "Say, I know how to make his supper more enjoyable. I'll tell him another story. Remember the one about the turkey? No one hearing that can stay sober!"

Dave strolled over again and reached to pull out the chair. It wouldn't budge. Dave gave it another pull and realized that the stranger's foot was hooked around its leg, holding the chair in place.

"Hey, this chair seems to be stuck." Yanking the chair hard, Dave freed it and sat down. "Your foot was in the way. Makes a body think you're unfriendly. Of course, I know better than that."

Dave leaned forward and set his hands on the table-top near the bread. Suddenly the stranger's hand shot out, plunging his scalping knife into the slices and nailing them to the table. Dave could hear a low rumble vibrating deep in the man's chest. It reminded him of a snarling dog guarding a bone. Dave's eyes popped. Then the man concentrated on his plate again.

Dave recovered quickly. "Like bread, do ya? I like bread too. Mind you, I wouldn't kill a body for it, but it does go well with stew. It's good stew too. Mrs. Ford is a good cook."

The man didn't look up but continued shoveling it in with both hands, dunking bread in to sop up the gravy. It all disappeared through an opening in his hairy face—just about where his mouth should be, Dave reckoned.

"Ya haven't et in polite company for a while, have ya, mister?" No answer. Dave continued. "Where ya from? I bet you're from Pennsylvania. Ya look like ya come a far piece. Ya know"—he leaned forward—"you can get yourself a bath for five cents at the back of the fort." The stranger stopped chewing, and his eyes flicked up. "Shave too." He looked steadily at Dave. "Five cents," Dave repeated.

"Did I ever tell ya the story about the turkey in a bush? Well, just relax, and let me tell ya it."

The other customers nudged one another. They all knew the story well and looked forward to witnessing the stranger's enjoyment of it.

The stranger made an indescribable noise of ire, as if he was in torment, as he started to eat faster, bolting down the food. His big teeth closed down hard on the bowl of the spoon as if he could eat that too.

"Take it easy, mister, there's more stew. Now, where was I?" Dave got comfortable and began. "Not too long ago, I was out huntin'. Close to the fort, ya know? Not too many Injuns hereabouts, them bein' so a-feared of me. But there's always one tryin' to think he can out-smart Dave Merrill, Injun-whupper. And that's what happened that day. I was just roamin' around, thinkin' thoughts of pheasants and ducks. Who'd a known that on this day I'd come upon one of the trickiest fowl ya ever did see? Did ya ever hear of a fowl shootin' back? I never did neither. So ya just set back and open your ears a bit wider, and I'll tell ya all about this puzzlin' question." Dave looked eagerly for a response but got nothing. The stranger kept right on eating. "That's right—you guessed it. That fowl weren't no fowl at all. It was an Injun!" Dave laughed delightedly at how he was bedazzling his listener and continued.

"Me and Laurier and some others were walkin' in the woods when I heard this low, gobblin' noise. Naturally I got to thinkin' it was a turkey, and I surely did relish the sound of that. Betwixt you and me, ain't nothin' like roast turkey—except maybe stew. I can see you're mighty partial to that." He shook his head in pleasant reminiscence. "I spied the bush where all that noise was a-comin' from, and I commenced to creep closer. I heard that old bird a-gobblin' and seen that bush a-shakin', and I thought, 'Sure as hell, there's my supper.' But as I started stalkin' that bird—ya see that?" Dave interrupted himself, pointing with one finger to the nape of his neck. The man didn't look up. "Every time there's an Injun around, that hair at the nape just stands up on end like pig bristles. And it was a-standin' then! And I knew"—he moved closer—"I knew that there was no turkey in that bush." Dave waited for a startled reaction but got none.

"So, bein' crafty, I make a big deal of sendin' Laurier out a ways, pretending to be a-huntin'. While I"—he jabbed his finger into his chest—"ducked down and backed outta there. Then I circled around behind where that bird ought to be. That's when I spied him. There was this here red devil just a-squattin' and a-gobblin' and a-tuggin' on a rope tied to that bush. He made so much noise, I thought he was gonna lay a couple of eggs! He had his rifle in his other hand, waitin' for Laurier to come look for that bird. He had his beady eyes on him so much, he didn't see me at all!

"So as I watched that bush a-shakin' and that 'turkey' a-gobblin' I just raised my gun and shot into them tail feathers. Well, that there Injun was dead on the spot. Killt him in mid-gobble!

"Come to think on it, that Injun looked almost as surprised as that feller that had the cow fall on him. And now there's two widdas who can't show their faces around the council fires." He sat back modestly, awaiting

praise. People all around laughed and watched hopefully for a similar reaction. But no laughter issued from
the hunter. He was as wood.

Finished eating, the man finally looked up and
stared, stiff-faced, at Dave for several long seconds. His
tongue whipped out the lower half of his face and
licked away the gravy. Then he ran his sleeve across his
mouth and sucked his teeth loudly. Some crumbs were
caught in his beard.

"Ya missed those." Dave pointed. "It don't matter
none, I guess. It kinda blends in with the other bits of
meals hangin' in your beard. Gives ya a well-traveled
look. A little somethin' from everywhere."

The man's eyes rolled wildly. For a second Dave expected steam to come a-whistling out of his ears like a
kettle on the boil.

Slamming his hands down on the table, the stranger
leaped to his feet, sending his chair crashing to the floor
behind him and making the table shiver. His face turned
purple, nostrils flared and eyes bugged out. He reached
into his pocket and pulled out a clenched fist. The room
quieted. Dave looked at it, a trifle alarmed; then it
opened up, and he slapped a coin down hard on the
table.

Dave was irked. "Now, lookee here, mister! You
been a-settin' there, eatin' and drinkin' and not even
tryin' to be friendlylike. I don't like it. You come to
civilization, ya ought to at least talk to people." Dave

sprang to his feet. "I'll fight ya. I killt many an Injun. I guess I can lick one ornery mountain man." Dave stuck out his chin aggressively.

The stranger, watching Dave like an old buffalo watches the antics of a calf, picked up his axe and ran his thumb consideringly along its shiny, curved blade. He rumbled, and his whole body shook with suppressed fury, as if something deep inside him was about to explode.

Staring at Dave in a frenzy, he rasped out, "You're a real funny man, ain't ya? I hate funny men. Knew me one once'st. But only once'st!"

Suddenly he swung up his axe. As it arced dangerously through the air, sparks of light shot off its razor-sharp blade. With mighty strength, it was flung back over the man's powerful shoulder, ready to be plunged at the "funny man" standing across from him.

Ford groaned. The crowd gasped. A shocked Dave stood, mouth agape, waiting for the angry blade to descend on his innocently good-humored head. He waited . . . the room waited . . . Ford waited . . .

But it never came down.

"I'm goin' someplace where I can find some peace and quiet!" the stranger ground out. Then his bent arm relaxed, allowing the axe to rest back across his shoulder. Grabbing up his sack and rifle, he stomped out of the room.

Dave exhaled nervously. Everyone sighed in relief.

"Whoa, Dave, that was close! I told ya he was salty!"

"Ford, I ain't payin' that no never mind. Truth is, I just brightened up that feller's day somethin' awful. I knew he didn't dislike me as much as he pretended to. I seen a little twinkle in his eyes as that blade come up. Why, he'd as soon take an axe to his own mother!"

Sometime later, Monty came running in, all excited. "Say, did ya see that big mountain man that just left?"

"I seen him and had him to tea," Dave affirmed breezily.

"He just brought in forty Injun scalps in that sack of his. He's at the fort to get the bounty on 'em."

"Forty!" Ford exclaimed. "Why, he's almost as good as you are, Dave," Ford said innocently.

Dave came back. "But were they all in one encounter?"

"He didn't say," Monty replied. "He did say he wanted to take one more scalp, only he was eatin' at the time and couldn't be bothered." Everyone looked at Dave. "Sure wish't I'd seen him. I always wanted to meet Daniel Boone!"

Dave blanched and fell back into his chair.

"What's the matter, Dave? Ya look a bit green." Monty was concerned.

Dave stood up. Everyone eyed him. "I'm goin' home to Angie. I didn't get around to tellin' her about that there cow." He clapped his hat on. "'Tain't fair to deprive her of it." With that, he shuffled out the door, head held high. He had broken bread with Daniel Boone! Another story in the making.